Just friends . . .

"It must have been really tough for you to leave all your friends in the middle of high school," Rich said.

I nodded. "You don't know how tough," I said. "I can't stand being stuck out here in nowhereville."

"Indian Valley probably isn't as exciting as New York. But we have a lot of fun here—dances and rallies and stuff like that. We've got a homecoming-Halloween dance coming up. Want to come?" he asked.

Was this a general invitation or was he inviting me as his date? I wondered about the dating rituals of Wyoming people. If I accepted his offer, would I be officially known as Rich's girl?

I decided to play it safe. "Uh . . . I don't think so. But thanks," I said. "I left the most wonderful boyfriend in the world in New York. I don't think he'd want me going to dances with other guys."

"Just as a friend," Rich promised. He sounded hurt. "I was just trying to be friendly, seeing as how you don't know anybody around here yet. Don't you want to fit in and have a good time?"

"No, I don't. I didn't want to come here in the first place. My dad promised me that he'd let me go back to New York if I'm still unhappy in June. So I intend to be miserable all year."

Rich looked at me strangely. "I'd say that was a dumb plan. Why don't you try and make the best of your situation?"

"And I suppose you think you're the best that Indian Falls has to offer," I snapped.

"You said it, not me."

Don't miss any of the books in *Love Stories*
—the romantic series from Bantam Books!

The Boy Next Door

Janet Quin-Harkin

BANTAM BOOKS
NEW YORK • TORONTO • LONDON • SYDNEY • AUCKLAND

RL 6, age 12 and up

THE BOY NEXT DOOR
A Bantam Book / June 1995

Produced by Daniel Weiss Associates, Inc.
33 West 17th Street
New York, NY 10011

ISBN: 0-553-56663-6

Published simultaneously in the United States and Canada

Bantam Books are published by Bantam Books, a division of Bantam
Doubleday Dell Publishing Group, Inc. Its trademark, consisting of the
words "Bantam Books" and the portrayal of a rooster, is Registered in
U.S. Patent and Trademark Office and in other countries. Marca
Registrada. Bantam Books, 1540 Broadway, New York, New York 10036.

PRINTED IN THE UNITED STATES OF AMERICA

OPM   0   9

To Elise Howard and ten years working together.

Chapter One

MUSIC WAS SPILLING out into the hallway as Suzanne and I stepped out of the elevator onto the twentieth floor. I could feel the thump of the beat through the soles of my shoes. I could also feel my heart thumping, almost as loudly.

"I can't believe we're actually here!" I whispered, grabbing Suzanne's arm for support. "We're really going to Brendan's party."

"And if things progress the way I think they will," Suzanne said knowingly, "I'd say this is the start of a beautiful relationship. Amber and Brendan, a match made in heaven—and helped along by Suzanne Altman, of course."

"Hmph," I muttered, giving her a look that made her laugh. But I couldn't stop smiling to myself. It was all too good to be true. I'd started high school a year earlier at Dover Prep, an exclusive and academically strong private school in Manhattan, as a short, shy nobody. I'd been fourteen years old and looked about eleven. In fact, the only thing I'd had going for me that year was my skill in gymnastics, which nobody at Dover knew about anyway. I'd gazed with envy at all those girls with perfect bodies who confidently swept down the halls in the latest fashions. Then, toward the end of the year, things had started to happen to me. I'd grown. I'd filled out in all the right places. It had put an end to my gymnastic hopes, but people at school had started to notice I was alive. The turning point came when I had rescued Suzanne's heel from a grating and helped her to her apartment. After that we'd started walking home together. Suzanne was a live wire who knew everybody. Pretty soon I was part of her clique. And her clique included Brendan Cooper.

I'd been gazing at him longingly all freshman year, marveling at the length of his eyelashes, those adorable little creases in his cheeks when he smiled, and the way he looked at girls with his smoldering gaze. I'd never dreamed that that gaze would be turned on me, but at the start of sophomore year, we'd been made biology lab partners.

Talk about fate! We'd sat side by side at a lab bench, our knees touching as we peered at dissected worms. The teacher was serious and bespectacled, and he spoke in a way that made Brendan and me giggle. Brendan had started whispering funny things into my ear, and the feel of his lips and warm breath made me dizzy. I couldn't believe it when he suggested working on our bio homework together.

2

So we'd gone to Fiorelli's Coffeehouse on 75th Street, which was a favorite after-school hangout, and worked through biology assignments together. At first it had just been biology, but one day we sat over double mochas for hours, just talking and laughing. I'd never felt so at ease with a guy before, never been able to laugh and kid around. But Brendan was different. He was really funny, and he was great at imitating teachers. I'd noticed other people watching us and I felt really proud to be with him. I could have sat there with him forever.

"I had a really fun time today, Amber," Brendan had said as he walked me home. "We should do this again."

And then it had happened. Outside my building he'd given me a gentle good-bye kiss. Even though it was a mere brushing of our lips, and there were people passing all around us, it had made me tingle right down to my toes.

A week later we'd been at Fiorelli's again when he told me about his party. "It will be cool," he'd said. "My folks will be out of town."

"And they're letting you have a party while they're gone?"

"Not exactly," he'd said, his eyes twinkling mischievously. "My sister's home from college. She's supposed to be keeping an eye on me, but she's cool. And she'll be useful for buying the beer. You will come, won't you?" He had reached out and covered my hand with his.

"Sure," I'd told him. "I wouldn't miss it." I'd

3

known then that I'd be at that party, even if it meant swimming the Atlantic Ocean to get there. Actually it meant something almost as tough—convincing my parents. My parents are surprisingly old-fashioned for hip New Yorkers. I knew exactly what they'd do if I asked them for permission to go to Brendan's party. They'd call Brendan's parents and discover that they weren't planning to be home. Then they'd tell me, in their calm, reasonable voices, that they were sorry, but I wasn't allowed to go to a party with no adult chaperons.

I had called Suzanne in despair. "I just have to go," I'd said. "He told me it wouldn't be any fun if I wasn't there. I think he really likes me, Suzanne. I can't miss this."

"It's simple." Suzanne's deep, mellow voice had come down the line. "If you think your parents will say no, then don't tell them."

"Wait a minute, Suzanne," I'd said, laughing uneasily. "I can't lie to my parents. And I'd have to come up with a pretty good story to be allowed to stay out after midnight. . . ."

"So tell them you're spending the night at my house," Suzanne had said. "You can come back with me after the party, so it won't even be a lie."

"Suzanne, you're a genius!" I'd said excitedly into the phone. My parents wouldn't object to my sleeping over at my best friend's house on a Friday night.

"Great. I can't wait for Friday night!" Suzanne had said.

It had all been so easy. Friday night I had smuggled out my new black velvet dress, for which I'd spent way more than I should have, and everything else I needed

4

to make myself look cool, cute, and desirable for Brendan. I'd gone to Suzanne's and changed my clothes. And there I was, walking toward his door.

It was Brendan himself who opened the door. His face lit up when he saw me. "Wow, Amber—looking good!" he said, his eyes traveling from my head down to my high-heeled shoes. He took my hand. "Come out onto the balcony."

"We just got here," I giggled to Suzanne, "and he's already trying to lure me away."

"I want to show you something," he said, his dark eyes gazing into mine. "You'll never believe it."

I followed him across the living room and out onto the balcony. Central Park was a huge rectangle of darkness surrounded by a million lights.

"How about that?" Brendan said, waving proudly.

"The view? It's pretty—"

"Not the view," he said. "In the corner!"

I looked over. "A keg!" I exclaimed. "How did you get it up here?"

"It wasn't easy," he said. "Thomas and Keith and I brought it up in the service elevator in a garbage can. My sister bought it for us. Pretty cool, right?"

That was one of the things I liked about Brendan. He took risks. I hoped a little of his cool would rub off on me. It wasn't easy trying to grow up cool with overprotective parents like mine. The thought of them shot a jolt of guilt through me. I'd never lied to them before—at least not about something as big as this. This was major deception.

I didn't have time to think about it any longer,

because Brendan put his arms around me. "And while I've got you all to myself out here . . ." he whispered. Then he kissed me. It wasn't our first kiss. He'd kissed me when we walked home from the coffeehouse together. But we'd had to break off because people were looking. This time we were alone in the darkness and his lips felt warm and wonderful. Through the fabric of my dress I could feel his warm hands on my back and his heart hammering against mine.

"We should probably go back inside," I whispered, laughing nervously as we drew apart again. "Everyone will be wondering where we are."

"No, they won't," he said. "They're not stupid. They'll be able to guess where we are and what we're doing."

From the darkness came the muted honking of taxicabs and a burst of jazz music. "I love New York," I sighed. "It's so romantic and exciting."

"Yeah," Brendan said, his arms still around my waist. "I couldn't live anywhere else."

"Me neither, although my parents keep talking about escaping to a barn in Connecticut."

"They're just fantasizing," Brendan said. "All New Yorkers do it. My mom's always threatening to move out to the Hamptons, but she doesn't really mean it."

"You're right," I said. "My parents love the city, too."

"Hey, Brendan, get in here," a voice yelled from inside. "There are some guys at the door who say they know you from soccer camp."

"It must be Danny!" Brendan yelled. He let go of me. "To be continued later," he whispered in my ear,

6

and dragged me back into the room. Brendan was soon noisily greeting the guys at the front door, and I found myself swallowed up in the crowd.

"I didn't see you arrive, Amber," Mandy Blake said. Mandy was also in Suzanne's group and had become a friend of mine, too.

"That's because Brendan dragged her outside the moment she got here," Suzanne said, grinning.

"What for, to admire the view?" Alicia asked.

"What do you think for, stupid?" Suzanne said. She rolled her eyes at me. "So I guess you two really are an item. I heard a guy calling you Brendan's hot new babe."

I felt my cheeks getting warm as the other girls looked at me with interest. Lauren, a popular junior, was looking at my dress.

"You got that in the Village, didn't you?" she asked. "I saw it in the window of a store on Eighth Street, but I couldn't afford it."

"I decided I'd rather go naked for the rest of the year and get it," I said, grinning delightedly. "My mother would flip if she knew what I paid for it."

"What are charge cards for?" Suzanne joked.

"Looks good on you," Lauren agreed.

"You can borrow it sometime if you want," I said, feeling generous.

"Thanks," she said, smiling.

It felt great to be the center of attention, getting admiring glances—and having a real conversation with some of Dover's most popular students. In a few minutes, Brendan appeared with a beer for me. I took a sip, although I'm not much of a drinker. I hate the taste of beer.

The room was filling up and some kids were smoking, filling the air with a blue haze. The noise level rose with the smoke. Someone had put on a rap CD, and kids were dancing in the hallway. The music was so loud, it was like being part of a giant heartbeat.

"What if someone calls the cops, Brendan?" Mandy asked.

"Don't worry. I squared it with all the neighbors. Everyone on this floor is out for the evening and the old guy down below doesn't care. I slipped twenty bucks to the super, so that's okay. Everything's under control." He pulled me to him and gave me a quick peck on the cheek.

"So you managed to get here without your parents giving you any grief, Amber?" Mandy asked.

"We told them she was sleeping over at my place," Suzanne said.

"Actually it was easy," I said. "They were hardly paying attention when I asked them. They've had a lot on their minds recently . . . my dad's got this big case coming up in court and my mom has to do a presentation for a new account at work, and right in the middle of all this they got a call from my grandfather out in Wyoming, saying that he's broken his leg and he can't take care of the ranch. So now they're trying to decide what to do about him—"

"You have a grandfather on a ranch, Amber?" interrupted Thomas, one of Brendan's friends. "Somehow you don't seem like the type."

8

"I am absolutely not the type," I said. "Neither is my dad. He couldn't wait to get away from there when he went to college."

"I don't know," Alicia commented. "I think a ranch sounds romantic. All those horses. Do you ever go there?"

"We haven't been there since I was a little kid," I said. "My dad and my grandpa don't get along. Grandpa can't understand Dad's need for the city life. And I don't have the greatest memories of the place. I remember this boy who'd tried to kiss me in my grandfather's hayloft. I also remember him putting a frog down my back when we were hiking near the river, and my grandfather saying I was spoiled rotten because I freaked out during a thunderstorm. Not the greatest vacation I've ever had."

Someone put on a new rap CD, and we all started dancing. But I felt a little guilty. I wanted to be loud and carefree like my friends, but I couldn't shake off the dumb feeling of guilt. Was I the only one who felt that way? As Suzanne had said, I hadn't lied to my parents. I just hadn't mentioned all the facts. People did stuff like that all the time. My friends thought it was no big deal. So why did I feel bad?

I grabbed Brendan as he came past. "Dance with me," I begged. Almost on cue, the music changed to a slow beat.

Brendan pulled me close. His cheek was warm against mine and his arms were wrapped around me so tightly that we were breathing as one. I closed my eyes with a feeling of perfect, utter contentment. It

9

was the most wonderful night of my life. I didn't ever want it to end.

We didn't even hear the doorbell at first.

"See if it's crashers, dude," Brendan called to Thomas, who was standing near the door, sipping a beer. "If it's the old guy complaining, be nice to him."

"Thanks for letting me handle it," Thomas called back sarcastically, but he opened the door anyway. Brendan kissed my forehead and we started to sway to the music. We were really getting into a rhythm when Thomas pushed through the crowd to reach us.

"Hey, Amber," he said worriedly. "It's your mom and dad. And they don't look very happy!"

Chapter Two

"**M**OM, DAD, WHAT are you doing here?" I said with phony brightness. I had a sinking feeling in the pit of my stomach, but I wasn't going to let them make a scene in front of my friends.

"The question is, what are *you* doing here, Amber?" my dad said angrily. "You told us you were spending the night at Suzanne's."

"I was . . . I mean, I am," I stammered. "I was over at Suzanne's, and then Brendan called and suggested that we drop in for a little while. . . ."

"And you just happened to have a velvet dress with you? How convenient," my mother said, giving me a withering stare. "You know our rules, Amber. You do not go to parties without permission—"

"Mom, please, chill," I whispered. Everyone was staring at us.

"Get your things. You're leaving with us."

11

"The rest of my things are at Suzanne's."

"Not anymore they're not. We collected them when we stopped at Suzanne's to give you the plastic bag you dropped in the hallway. We thought you wouldn't want to spend the night without your eyedrops and toothbrush, so we went by on our way home from the Chinese restaurant."

She waited for me to say something, but there wasn't anything I could think of to say. Brendan had pushed his way though the crowd. "Is something the matter, Amber?" he asked.

"I have to go home," I said, biting my lip because I certainly wasn't going to cry in front of him and all those people.

"Hey, what a bummer," he said, his eyes holding mine in silent sympathy. "I'll call you, okay?"

"Okay," I muttered. I turned to follow my parents down the hallway. My little brother and sister were waiting in the hall. People moved back to give us room. I'd never been so humiliated in my life.

"Mom, Dad," I began.

My father turned around to look at me with a cold, calm expression.

"Not another word, Amber. We've had a long day, and we're tired. We'll talk about it in the morning. You'll go straight to your room when we get home."

I climbed into the backseat of the taxi my father hailed, and we drove home in silence.

The next morning my parents were already sitting at the breakfast table when I came into the kitchen.

12

"Sit down, Amber," my mother said, waving at a seat. It was like being the prisoner at a trial.

"I'm really sorry," I began. I've always found that groveling works well. No parent can stay mad at their kid if she admits she's pond scum and begs to be forgiven. "I want you to know that this is the first time I've ever done anything like this, and I didn't feel too good about it." I looked hopefully from one parent to the other, trying to judge whether I was reaching them or not. They were both listening in silence.

"Do you know what it's like to be the only one who can't go to a party?" I continued. "Everyone thinks you're a geek! You both chose this school for me—it's very, very social. There are parties every weekend. . . ."

The silence remained as my excuses trailed off, and it hung there in the air until I began to feel really uncomfortable. My father cleared his throat. "I realize the initial mistake might have been ours, Amber," he said. "Yes, we were the ones who selected Dover for you. It's a very good school. Unfortunately it's also a school for spoiled, rich brats, and that's not what we want for you."

"You're not going to make me transfer, are you?" I said in a panic. "Not when I'm finally beginning to fit in for the first time in my life. Not when I've finally met a boy who likes me, and gotten a good part in the play—"

"Honey, we only want what's best for you in the long run," Mom said calmly. "And unsupervised parties and drinking are not what's best."

13

"But, Mom," I started to protest. She held up her hand and looked at my father.

"We'd better call Beau and Katie in here and let them know what's going on, too."

"Why do they need to see me get in trouble?" I demanded. "You know what Beau's like. He'll remember everything you say and he'll repeat it word for word whenever he gets mad at me."

"We want them in here because this concerns them too," Dad said. He put his head around the door. "Get in here, you two," he called. "Turn the TV off."

We heard muffled complaints, and then two tousled heads appeared. "It was my favorite Muppet Babies cartoon," Katie complained.

"Sit," my father said, indicating stools at the kitchen counter. There was something in his voice that made them both sit without arguing.

"Your mother and I have been up most of the night talking," Dad said.

"You're not going to get a divorce, are you?" Katie asked. "I don't want to go to court and be in a custody battle, like Amy."

"We're not getting divorced, Katie," Dad said. "Just be quiet and listen and you'll find out what we've decided."

He waited until we were all perfectly still before he began. He's not a lawyer for nothing. "Your mother and I are not very happy about the way things are going for this family. You three are having problems—"

"I said I was sorry," I butted in. "I said it wouldn't happen again."

"It's not just you, Amber," Dad said with a glance at Mom. "Beau gets his lunch money stolen. Katie's school psychologist says she has problems interacting with her peer group and wants her to come in for therapy three days a week. Your lying to us, Amber, was just the last straw."

"And the crazy thing is, we really thought we were doing our best for you," Mom interrupted. "We pay a fortune in tuition to send you all to the best schools, but we realize that's not the answer. What you need is our time and attention, and we can't give it to you, because we're both too busy working our tails off."

"We need time to be a family, kids." Dad sighed. "This is no way to live—always rushing to meet deadlines, always under pressure, never eating meals together, pizza instead of home-cooked food—"

"But I like pizza," Katie interrupted.

"The things we like aren't always the best for us, honey," Mom said softly. "We're your parents. We have to think about what's really best for you, so that you grow up happy and healthy."

There was a dramatic pause.

"Are we going to public schools, Daddy?" Beau asked at last.

"Probably. We'll have to look into it, but I'd say probably," Dad said.

Mom took a deep breath. "The decision we've come to is that New York City is not a healthy place to bring up a family," she said, "and at the rate we're going, your father and I will both be candidates for heart attacks by the time we're forty. I know you've been hearing us

15

talk about your grandfather's problem all week. He's broken his leg and has nobody to help him keep the ranch going. Last night Daddy and I decided that the right thing would be to go take care of him."

"In Wyoming?" I blurted out.

"In Wyoming," my father said.

"All of us? For how long?" I heard my voice quiver as I said it.

"Who knows?" Dad said. "Maybe forever. We'll just have to see how things work out there."

I jumped up. "Forever? Dad, you can't be serious. We can't move away from New York."

"We've been talking about it for some time now," Mom said.

"I know, the barn in Connecticut," I said, "but I didn't think you were serious. I thought you liked New York as much as I do."

"We're tired of our stressful lives," Dad said. "And as your mom said, we've come to the conclusion that New York is no place to raise a healthy family."

I jumped up from my stool. "You *can't* be serious! I can't leave New York now. All my friends are here. Couldn't I move in with Suzanne? They've got an extra bedroom while her brother is at college. I know her mom would say yes—"

My father held up his hand. "Suzanne is a major part of the problem, Amber. Her mother gives her all kinds of freedoms we don't want for you."

My mom interrupted. "It's mainly because of you that we came to this decision," she said. "You're the one we want out of the city as soon as possible."

"I can't believe you're doing this!" I wailed. "It's child abduction. It's child abuse. I'll go to the juvenile authorities and see what they've got to say about this!"

Dad grinned. "They'll say that a child has to move with her family until she turns eighteen," he said. "Like it or not, you're coming with us, Amber."

"And I think you will like it, kids," Mom said. There was real excitement in her voice. "Imagine not having to battle the traffic and crowds every day. We could get horses for you if you wanted. We'd have time to eat dinner together."

"But how will you be able to find a job in Wyoming?" I scoffed.

"I'm not taking a job," Mom said simply, "and neither is your father. We're both quitting work."

"Oh, no," Katie wailed. "We'll be homeless and on welfare. I don't want to sleep in a cardboard box!"

This broke the tension and we had to laugh, but it raised a serious question. "What will we live on?" I asked.

"We'll do just fine," Mom said, with a glance at Dad. "We'll start out with Grandpa on the ranch until he's well again, and if things don't work out with him, then maybe we'll get a place of our own. One thing about living here—we've been paid fairly well, and we've saved quite a bit. And in Wyoming, we won't have ridiculously high rent or private-school tuition to pay. I'm sort of looking forward to raising our own vegetables and fruit, and it will give Dad time to do what he's always dreamed of."

"What's that?" I asked.

"Write a novel," Mom said.

17

I stared across at Dad. He actually blushed. "It's always been my secret dream," he said softly. "And if it doesn't work out, if we find that I can't write a best-seller and we can't grow our own food, then I'm sure there's always work for a lawyer, or I could teach at a local college. There are plenty of options."

"For you, maybe," I said, "but what's in it for me?"

"Meeting a bunch of kids whose values haven't been screwed up," Mom said. "Realizing that money doesn't buy happiness. A chance to let you grow up as your own person and not a sophisticated phony. Who knows what talents you'll discover when you have a chance to try new things?"

"Sure," I said bitterly, "butter churning and cow milking."

"Cows?" Katie asked excitedly. "Are we going to live with cows?"

Mom smiled at Katie's excited little face. "You can have as many pets as you like, honeybun—cows, sheep, pigs, rabbits . . . whatever you want."

Katie slid down from her stool. "I'm going to pack my things," she said. "Can we go tomorrow?"

"Not tomorrow," my father said, lifting Katie into his arms, "but real, real soon. As soon as we can get a tenant for this place and make all the arrangements. I can't wait to see my partners' faces when I tell them I'm quitting."

I looked from Dad's excited face to Mom's to Katie's. At least Beau didn't look overjoyed. Perhaps

18

he was remembering that he'd thrown up when Grandpa made him eat homegrown turnips.

I felt a big sob coming. "I can't believe you guys," I said through the lump in my throat. "I can't believe you'd do this to me. I won't go. I'll find a way to stay here if it's the last thing I do!"

Chapter Three

I WAS SO upset I wouldn't even talk to Brendan or Suzanne when they called later that day. My father poked his head in my room to tell me that the gang was still planning to go to the Italian film festival that afternoon, and that I could meet them there or at Fiorelli's afterward.

"So what did you tell them? That I was grounded until I'm safely among the herds of buffalo?" I snapped.

My father grinned. "You can meet your friends if you want to, Amber. We're not monsters, you know."

I decided against the Italian movie. I knew it was about a woman who falls in love with a soldier who goes away and gets killed in a war, and I had a horrible feeling that I might sob all the way through it. But I did manage to splash cold water on my face and put on some lipstick so that I looked human enough to join them at Fiorelli's.

My friends were sitting in a corner booth when I walked in, and they looked at me with compassion. Mandy scooted over to make room for me next to Brendan.

"You missed a good movie, Amber. It was so sad," she said.

I managed a halfhearted smile as I squeezed in beside Brendan.

"You must be in serious trouble," Suzanne ventured. "Your dad was like Mr. Iceberg when I called this morning."

"Yeah, he told me you weren't talking to anyone," Brendan said. "I'm sorry you got in so much trouble, Amber. I had no idea your parents would freak out about a little party."

I tried to answer him, but I had to hold back a sob instead. I looked around Fiorelli's, noticing the Italian opera posters on the walls, the pink candles on the tables, and the Pavarotti playing in the background, drowning out the impatient roar of the traffic outside. Lights were glowing from a marquee across the street. There was a kebab vendor on one corner and David's Deli, home of David's Famous Pastrami, on the other. This was New York, and I loved it.

"Are you in real trouble now?" Brendan asked, touching my hand gently. "I mean, are they grounding you or what?"

"Worse than that," I began. "They're taking me to Wyoming."

"They're what? For how long?" My friends were all looking at me in shock.

"Forever," I said sadly.

"I don't believe it," Brendan said. "You break one tiny rule and they ship you off to Wyoming?"

"You'd better believe it, because it's true," I said. "My parents said they've been worrying about what to do with my grandfather, and this helped them come to a decision."

"Just because of your grandfather?" Mandy snapped. "You don't just up and move to Wyoming because some old guy has broken his leg!"

"That's only part of the reason," I said. "They want to get us out of the city and to a place where life is simple."

"You've got to be kidding," Alicia said, rolling her eyes.

"They can't do that, Amber," Suzanne said calmly, tossing back her hair. "Go to the child advocate at school. Tell her your rights are being abused. You have rights, too, you know."

"And psychiatrists have proven that it's harmful to move a student in the middle of high school," Alicia agreed. "They'd actually be risking your mental health, Amber."

"The Constitution guarantees life, liberty, and the pursuit of happiness," Thomas added. "I'd say you have zero chance of pursuing happiness in Nebraska or wherever it is."

"Wyoming," I said.

"Same difference," Thomas said. "Once you get past Pennsylvania there's nothing until you reach California. I've driven cross-country once. Trust me."

"Wyoming's okay," Alicia commented. "Jackson Hole looks cool. I've seen it on *Lifestyles of the Rich and Famous.* They have natural hot springs and horse-drawn sleigh rides. Tons of celebrities go there."

"We could come out and visit you for a skiing vacation," Suzanne said, looking enthusiastic all of a sudden. "I'd love to lie in a hot spring with snow all around. How romantic!"

"We're not going to Jackson Hole," I said bitterly. "We're going to a place way in the boonies that nobody's ever heard of. We're going to live on a ranch. It's the worst thing that could happen to anybody!"

They were back to looking sorry for me again.

"So just refuse to go," Suzanne said. "What can they do, carry you off over their shoulders?"

"My dad says that children under eighteen have to go with their parents, whether they like it or not," I said.

"Not if you make a big enough fuss," Mandy said. "When I can't get my own way, I threaten not to eat. My parents are so worried I'll turn into an anorexic, they always give in."

"I've only got a couple of weeks before we leave," I said. "I don't think I could starve myself to death in that amount of time."

"Just run away," Suzanne said, as if this were the simplest thing in the world. "We'd hide you, wouldn't we, guys?"

Brendan gave me a sweet, wicked smile. "You could always share my room, Amber. You know that."

"No, seriously," Suzanne said. "If you don't want to go, don't. You're almost grownup. You can live

23

with one of us. We'll hide you until they're gone."

I shook my head. "I couldn't do that," I said. "They'd be worried sick about me."

"They deserve it, not caring about your happiness," Mandy said. "I mean, Wyoming is worse than a death sentence. You'll die of boredom there."

"Think about it, Amber," Suzanne said. "No stores within a million miles, no coffeehouses, and you'll have to go square dancing with guys who wear big boots." She paused and started laughing. "And you'll have to learn to say *hee-haw* and *wooee!*"

"Believe me," I said, "I don't intend to get close enough to any Wyoming guy to dance with him, and I will never say *hee-haw*. In fact, I'm planning to lie in my bed and stare at the ceiling until they realize how unhappy I am. Then they'll have to send me back here."

Brendan was staring down at his cappuccino. Then suddenly he looked up with a big smile on his face. "Lighten up, Amber," he said. "You don't really think your parents will be able to stand it out there for more than a couple of months, do you? They're used to New York, too, remember. They might think it's cute to live on a farm for a couple of weeks, but wait until it snows and they're stuck five miles from town with only one channel on the TV. I bet you'll be back by Christmas."

I looked at him hopefully. "You really think so?"

He nodded. "I'm counting on it," he said. "Who else would I take to the winter formal?"

It was about the sweetest thing anybody had ever

24

said to me, and I felt dangerously near to tears again.

"I hope so," I said. "I just hope you're right."

I spent my last weeks in New York cramming in everything that I had always meant to do but never done. Brendan did everything with me, going to as many of our favorite hangouts and movie houses as possible. "So you don't die of culture starvation," he said.

What a great few weeks. Brendan and I really began to connect—to get to know each other. How was I ever going to leave him?

On my last day at Dover Brendan and I spent a perfect October day together. The temperature was warm without being muggy, and the leaves were beginning to turn gold on the trees in Central Park. We walked through the park together while horses clip-clopped by, pulling open carriages of tourists. Central Park had never looked lovelier. New York had never seemed a more perfect place to live. Central Park had always been just at the end of the block, and I'd hardly ever taken the time to walk through it. But that day I savored every tree, every rock, every fountain, saying to myself, *I'll never see this again.*

"I can't believe I'll be on the road to Wyoming in the morning," I said.

"I can't believe it, either," Brendan said. "We're only just getting to know each other and now you're going away. It's not fair."

"I'll never feel this way about anybody else," I blurted out.

"I know what you mean. You're really special,

25

Amber." He took my hand gently. "Saying good-bye is hard for me too."

"I'll think of you every day," I said. I felt a tear trickle down my cheek.

"Hey," he said, reaching across to wipe away the tear. "It's not like you're going to the end of the world. There are phones in Wyoming. I'll call you every night."

"That will cost a fortune."

"I don't care," he said. "My sister calls home from college all the time on our calling card. I should get equal privileges. And there are planes. I could hop a plane and come out to see you."

"You could?"

"Sure, or you could get your parents to fly you back here for vacations."

"Yeah," I said, a tiny glimmer of hope appearing in the darkness of my despair. "They'd have to allow me that, wouldn't they? They couldn't keep me away from my friends forever."

"And like I said," Brendan added, "when the first snow comes and the pipes freeze and they can't find fettuccine in the local store, I bet they'll run back to civilization. By next spring, you'll have forgotten that you were ever away. We'll go to all the new Broadway shows you've missed, and we'll go Rollerblading through Central Park when all the new leaves start growing back on the trees."

"Oh, Brendan, do you really think so?"

He smiled at me. "I'll be holding your hand, and when we come to a big tree like this one, I'll take you

26

in my arms and kiss you, just like this." His lips met mine, and we stood locked in each other's arms. "If you haven't forgotten all about me by next spring, that is," he teased as we drew apart. "If you haven't found a cowboy you like better by then!"

"Don't joke about things like that," I said angrily. "That will never happen."

We walked home, hand in hand. After a final good-bye kiss, I watched as he turned and slowly walked away. It was the last time I was going to see him for who knew how long. I wanted to remember the moment forever.

That night Dad came into my room as I was trying to cram the last of my stuff into an already-too-full duffel bag.

"Amber, I know you're mad at us for doing this to you," he said. "I know you don't want to go, but please believe we're doing what we think is best for all of us."

I went on trying to jam a pair of shoes into a non-existent space in the corner of the bag.

"Who knows?" he went on. "You might actually like it there."

"Right."

"You might even blossom into a person you never knew existed—one who doesn't need charge cards and expensive clothes and wild parties to have fun."

I got the shoes in and wrestled with the zipper.

"Your mother and I have been concerned about how much this has upset you," he went on, "and we've decided on a compromise."

27

I looked up hopefully.

"We've decided that you should give it a fair trial. If at the end of the school year you're still desperately unhappy in Wyoming, then we'll arrange to send you back to New York for your junior year. Does that sound fair?"

"It sounds better than nothing," I agreed. "Back to Dover?"

"I didn't say that. We'll have to think about it very carefully. But promise me that you'll give Wyoming a fair shot. It will be a challenge for all of us to adapt to a new way of life. We're going to need to pull together, okay, Amber?"

I gave a grunt, which could have meant okay, and he walked out of my room. But a new ray of hope was glimmering in my brain. If I could just survive the rest of the school year . . .

Chapter Four

"THIS WILL BE our closest town," Dad said as we pulled into Cody (population seven thousand). It looked very Wild West, as if Butch Cassidy and the Sundance Kid could come riding down Main Street at any moment. Cody had a couple of restaurants and quite a few motels.

We'd been driving for four days and had seen nothing except open space and lots of cows, and we were all getting tired. It had just started to rain, too. Everyone wanted to stop except for Dad, who was anxious to get to the ranch. He wouldn't even stop to let me see if there was a movie theater or a Gap, although I doubted there were any.

Katie was getting really whiny. She'd seen a sign that said Welcome to Cody, Gateway to Yellowstone National Park, and she was scared that she was going to have to live among the geysers and would be killed by super-hot steam. Beau started quoting statistics on the number of grizzly bear maulings there had been in Yellowstone recently. Even Mom looked back longingly at Jake's Roadhouse as we drove out of town.

"I suppose we should try to make it to Grandpa's before it gets dark," she said.

"The mountains are just ahead of us now," Dad said cheerfully.

"I don't see them," Beau muttered.

"That's because the clouds are low today. On a clear day you can see snowcapped peaks from here. It's a lovely sight," Dad said.

Nobody believed him. The whole world looked flat and gray. I had been trying to remember my last trip to see Grandpa. I didn't think the land had been flat and open; in fact, I remembered a lot of big trees that made scary noises when the wind blew. And there was a rushing river I'd fallen into once because I was trying to follow the boy who lived down the road—the one who'd put the frog down my back. I shivered as I remembered my panic at the cold, wriggling thing trapped inside my T-shirt. If that was what country hicks did for fun, then I'd better remember to wear high, tight necklines the entire time I was in Wyoming.

We left what was jokingly called the main highway and turned onto an even smaller one. The road started to climb. Soon trees appeared, and then a stream. Hills rose up, their slopes covered with a dark blanket of pine trees, and cows and horses grazed in the fields.

"Make sure you don't miss the turnoff this time," Mom warned Dad.

"I lived here for eighteen years," Dad reminded her.

"I know, but you missed it last time, remember? We wound up halfway up a mountain."

"It's right after the white picket fence," Dad said. "Just past the gas station."

The sign beside the road said Indian Falls, Pop. 625.

"Where's the town?" Beau asked suspiciously.

I was wondering the same thing. Through the rain I noticed a few houses surrounded by trees, some more horses, a white frame church, a general store, a hardware store advertising fishing tackle, a gas station with a couple of old cars standing outside, and a pretty two-story house with a picket fence.

"Is that it?" I asked.

"Pretty much," Dad said. "There are several communities like it along this road, and I understand they've built a couple of dude ranches, too."

"Wooee," I said, trying out my new vocabulary. "How exciting. I can't wait."

We turned off the highway and drove along a narrowing valley. The road was dirt, no longer pavement. It was really stormy now, with wind blowing the rain right into our windshield and making it hard to see what lay ahead.

"I'm cold. I want to go home," Katie wailed.

"Don't worry, pumpkin, we're almost there now," Dad said soothingly. "I bet your grandpa will have a big roaring fire going and a nice hot dinner waiting for us."

Trees swayed crazily above the road and Dad had to turn on the headlights in the fading light. Then

31

suddenly he said, "There it is. Home at last."

We bumped up a rutted driveway, between dark, swaying trees. In the gloom we could just make out the shape of a rambling farmhouse. A weak light was glowing in the downstairs windows. The house was pretty large and it looked like the loneliest place on earth. The wind howled as we parked the car and got out, almost blowing us away as we made it up the steps and onto the porch. That big roaring fire and hot meal sure sounded good right then.

The front door opened and light streamed out. A tall, muscular figure, his face hidden under a cowboy hat, came out onto the porch, then stood there, watching me as I was swept across the porch by a strong gust of wind. "Whoa!" I yelled as I fought to hang on to my purse and my CD carrier. As I regained my balance by clutching one of the porch posts, I noticed he wasn't wearing a cast on his leg. He was walking! It was all a mistake, and we could turn right around and go home!

"Grandpa!" I yelled. "You're walking. It's a miracle."

I could see white teeth gleaming in the headlights of our car. "Sorry to disappoint you, but it's not a miracle and I'm not your grandpa, although they do say I look mature for my age," said a young-sounding voice. I took another step toward him. When I was no longer blinded by the headlights I could see that he was a young cowboy, tall, fair-haired, and friendly-looking. He tipped his hat to me and pushed it back on his head in one gesture. "I'm Mr. Stevens's neighbor. My dad had me come over and see to his stock. I was figuring to stay and see if he needed help with his chores, but if he's got his family to take care of him now, I reckon I'll just take off for home. I'm sure you don't want any strangers hanging around. My name's Rich, by the way. And you are . . . ?"

"Amber," I said, trying to stop my teeth from chattering in the cold and wet.

"Amber." His face lit up. "I remember now. Boy, you've sure grown up since I saw you last. Amber, that was it. I knew it was something real pretty."

I was trying desperately to remember having met him before when suddenly the picture came back to my mind—the skinny boy hopping easily from rock to rock, calling out, "It ain't hard. Just follow me. Don't be scared." Then, as we'd sat side by side in the tall grass, he'd reached over to me and . . . "You were the one who put the frog down my back!" I exclaimed.

The grin spread clear across his face. "You remember that after all this time," he said, shaking his head. "Boy, did you holler something shocking. You'da thought I half killed you, the way you went running home to your ma. I thought I'd be in such big trouble I wouldn't be able to sit down for a week."

"And were you?" There was something very appealing about his easy grin, something that made me keep on talking to him even with the wind and rain swirling around us.

"Nah. Just got a whipping from my pa."

"Amber, come and give your mother a hand with these bags," my dad yelled.

"You need help?" Rich asked.

"It's okay. We can manage," I said. Somehow it

33

was important that he didn't think a family of wimps had arrived.

"I'll be off home, then," he said. "Your grandpa's sure looking forward to having y'all here with him. Be seeing ya around, then, Amber."

With that he vaulted the porch rail and disappeared into the night.

"Well, don't just stand there letting in all the cold air. Come on in," boomed a big voice. It was my grandpa, standing in the doorway with crutches under his arms. One leg was in plaster but otherwise he looked pretty much as I remembered—tall, broad, lots of white hair, and a white mustache. Scary-looking, in fact.

"What a night to arrive," he called out. "Haven't had rain in a couple of months. Everyone was complaining about the heat and the drought and now you bring this with you. Should hire yourselves out as rainmakers!"

Dad bounded up the steps to him. "How are you, Dad?"

"Not too bad, not too bad," Grandpa said. "Danged leg aches a bit, but otherwise I can't complain." I noticed that they didn't hug.

"Come inside," Grandpa instructed.

We followed Dad and Grandpa into the hallway.

"You remember Sylvia," my dad said, as if he were introducing my mom to a stranger.

Mom followed Dad up the steps and smiled shyly.

"And the kids," Dad said. "Amber, Beau, Katie. Say hi to your grandfather."

34

"Goodness gracious, don't tell me these are your children," Grandpa boomed. "Last time we saw each other they were knee-high to a grasshopper. You've been feeding them too much, Sylvia."

Katie had gone right up to him. "We got older, silly," she said, and he ruffled her hair.

Beau and I hung back, not so eager to make friends. "Hi, Grandpa," we mumbled.

"Beau, come here," Grandpa said. "I want to feel your muscles—see if you'll be any use to me roping calves this season."

Beau shot me a look of terror but went and had his arms inspected. "Mmm, you call these arms?" Grandpa said, shaking his head. "These are matchsticks. They wouldn't rope a jackrabbit. Have to put you to work right away to build them up."

His gaze passed on to me. "And this is Amber," he said. "Quite a young lady now, I see. Are you still afraid of your own shadow?"

"I never was afraid of my shadow," I said coldly.

He laughed. "Pretty much everything else," he said. "Spiders and thunder and cattle and frogs—"

"Only down my back," I said quickly.

I saw the amused glint in his eyes. "Did you catch young Rich Winter before he left? He's been taking care of my cattle for me. With my bad leg, I can't do it myself. He's been looking forward to seeing you again—collecting frogs all week."

"In which case," I said, tossing back my hair, "you'd better spread the word that any pea-brain around here who tries to come anywhere near me

35

with a frog is going to be more than sorry. I took ka-rate, and I'm not afraid to use it."

This made Grandpa roar. "Feisty little thing she's turned out to be," he said. "I like that." He looked at us, standing forlornly in the cold hallway. "Well, don't just stand there. Come on in."

We went through into the living room. "Sorry there's no heat," he said. "I don't ever get the oil de-livered for the central heating before November first, and I can't get outside to chop wood for a fire."

"That's okay. We'll be fine after a hot meal," Mom said.

"Take a look in the kitchen and see what you can find," Grandpa said. "I haven't been able to get out since they drove me home from the hospital, so sup-plies are a little low, I'm afraid."

The kitchen was charming, with all the fixings of a country home. A large table was in the center of a room with handmade curtains and lots of plants. It had everything. Except, of course, food. The pantry was almost empty. So was the fridge.

"I know, let's send out for pizza," Katie said brightly.

"Wasn't that the point of coming out here—to get away from take-out food and start eating home-cooked meals?" I pointed out.

"Well, how can we eat a home-cooked meal if there's no food to cook?" Dad said. "We'll just have to make do with one more night of take-out. I'll get the phone book."

Grandpa started laughing again. "Where do you

36

think you're going to get pizza delivered from, huh? This isn't New York City, you know."

I could have told him that. New York didn't have cold, damp houses miles away from civilization.

"Then I'll go out and get pizza for us," Dad said. "There must be some sort of take-out food—even frozen pizza from the grocery would do."

"They close at five o'clock," Grandpa said.

"Well, we need to eat something," Dad snapped, his good mood rapidly vanishing. "These kids have been sitting in the car all day. I'm going to drive until I find something."

We unloaded the car in the rain and watched Dad bump his way down to the road. "Take care, honey," Mom called after him, but I'm sure the wind was making too much noise for him to hear.

"I expect you'll want to get the sleeping arrangements fixed upstairs," Grandpa said. "I've been sleeping down here on the couch, on account of my leg, so I'll leave everything to you, Sylvia. You'll find clean sheets in the big linen closet in the hallway."

"I'll help you, Mom," I said.

"Me too," Beau and Katie both agreed, not wanting to be left downstairs with Grandpa.

We found several neatly stacked piles of sheets and made the beds together while the rain battered the windows and the wind howled around the gables. And still Dad didn't come. We went back downstairs and Beau began to cite possible causes of accidents in Wyoming. "Maybe a tree was struck by lightning and it fell on Dad's car. Maybe a cow jumped a fence and landed on Dad. Maybe there was a flash flood."

"Shut up, Beau," we all shouted, and he stopped for a while.

"Strange kids you've got there, Sylvia," Grandpa said, frowning at my mother.

"They're just tired and hungry, that's all," Mom said. "Where can Jake be?"

"We could watch some TV," Beau said. "*Jeopardy* should be on around now."

He jumped up, but Grandpa waved him back to his seat. "TV's not working right now," he said.

"The TV's not working?" Beau looked at Grandpa as if he'd said he never washed.

"Having no TV will be good for us," Mom said. "We've never had enough time to talk or to read, and I've always wanted to have the time to make things. Imagine having a homemade quilt on my bed, and knowing I'd sewn every stitch."

"My wife made the quilt that's on the bed in Jake's old room," Grandpa said. "She'd sit there in the evenings sewing it when he was a little boy."

I looked from one face to the next. It was true—my family was already slipping into a rural twilight zone. I had to stay normal for all their sakes.

"How can we rent videos if there's no TV?" I demanded. "I bet there's no movie theater closer than Cody."

Grandpa chuckled. "No video rental closer than that, either," he said. "Can't even say whether they stay open during the winter. Most things around here shut down after the tourist season. It's pretty quiet in the fall and winter."

"What do kids do for fun, then? Where do they hang out?"

"I guess they make their own fun," Grandpa said. "They like fishin' and they've got their horses for things like calf-roping contests. Most of them have to get up at the crack of dawn to do chores, so they don't stay up all hours of the night like city folk do."

I looked at him in openmouthed horror.

Mom looked at her watch. "It's nine-thirty," she said in a worried voice. "Do you think we should call the sheriff? Maybe Dad got lost."

At that moment the door burst open dramatically, sending in a flurry of dead leaves and cold, wet air. Dad stood there holding a box, dripping wet and wild-eyed. "There are no pizza parlors between here and Chicago," he shouted.

"I could have told you that, son," Grandpa said. "I was telling your good lady that everything closes after the tourist season."

"We were getting worried about you," Mom said, getting up to take the box from him and help him off with his wet jacket. "We thought you'd gotten lost."

"I thought you'd been struck by a falling tree, or that a cow jumped you," Beau added.

"Almost," Dad said. "It was wild out there, especially when I got back on the highway. I was nearly blown backward by that wind."

"So did you get us some pizza, Daddy?" Katie asked. "Did you find some in Chicago?"

39

"No, honey, I didn't find any pizza. In fact, I was lucky to find anything. There was one place in Cody that was still open, and they did me up a box of ribs and biscuits."

He opened the box and the warm, meaty smell filled the room. Suzanne had just convinced me that eating meat was morally wrong as well as unhealthy. I hesitated, torn between my principles and my desire not to starve. The smell was driving me crazy. The rest of my family had already started on the ribs and were devouring them like some Stone Age tribe. If I didn't act soon, there would be none left. My hunger won, and I grabbed a plate and piled it high with ribs. They were tender and juicy, tasting of wood smoke and with just enough tang. I was amazed how easily they slipped down.

After we'd eaten, Beau and Katie didn't need any urging to go to bed. It was, after all, past midnight in New York. In Wyoming we were in the Mountain Time zone, though. My parents and grandfather went to bed, too. I sat on the bed in my dad's old room, listening to the scary night noises and feeling very cold and alone. Quietly I opened my door so that the hall light shone in, and I got out a pen and some paper.

Dear Brendan, I wrote. *Well, I'm here and it's as bad as I thought it would be—no, make that worse. I can't imagine a more depressing place on the entire planet. Freezing cold, no TV, a cranky grandfather, and we're about as far out in the boonies as we could possibly be. The only neighbor is the kid who once put a frog down my back. Don't be sur-*

40

prised if you find me hammering on your front door within a week. . . .

I stopped writing because my hand was freezing and I couldn't go on. I snuggled down under the covers and pulled the homemade quilt over my head. The rain peppered the window and the wind howled. "I can't take it," I whispered over and over.

Chapter Five

I WOKE TO bright sunlight painting a stripe on my wall. The wall was papered with a faded rose pattern, which glowed in the sun. The air was definitely cold and crisp, but under my quilt it was toasty warm, so warm that I wasn't inclined to move. I swiveled my head around, taking in the details of the room. There was a closet in the corner, a battered old chest, and a good-looking desk with brass handles and a fold-down top against the wall. A hand-braided rug was on the floor, and the window was covered with lace curtains. It was all very folksy and I tried to imagine my sophisticated lawyer father ever living in this room. There was certainly no trace of his teenage personality in that room—no baseball pennants on the wall, no pictures of girls or dogs to reveal what kind of person he might have been.

I sat up enough to look out the window, still hugging the quilt to me, and gasped at what I saw. The sky was a deep, clear blue and the trees behind the house were a spectacular gold and red. Beyond them meadows stretched down to a tree-lined river and beyond that the mountains rose to peaks that were already white with snow. I wondered if it had snowed up there during the night. It certainly looked new, so white and dazzling in the sunlight that it almost hurt to look at it. And as I watched, a lone horseman came galloping across the fields. The horse's mane was streaming out in the wind and the cowboy sat easily on the horse. It was almost as if they were one creature. As they came closer I recognized the cowboy. It was Rich Winter, the guy who'd been collecting frogs to welcome me. I turned away, suddenly not so interested.

I smelled coffee brewing, and reached out to grab my robe. Grandpa was up, hobbling around the kitchen.

"Coffee's ready," he said, indicating a percolator on the stove.

"Thanks, but I don't drink coffee in the morning," I said.

"Don't drink coffee?" He looked appalled.

"Oh, I like a latte or a mocha with my friends at a coffeehouse, but not for breakfast."

He looked at me as if I were speaking a foreign language and shook his head. "I grew up with a nice strong cup to start the day and it hasn't hurt me none," he said. "So what do you usually have, tea?"

"Fresh-squeezed orange juice," I said. "We have a juicer at home."

"It's coffee or nothing today," he said. "I guess you're going to have to learn to change your fancy ways if you're going to live out here."

"I don't plan to stay longer than I have to," I said.

"Oh?"

"I didn't want to come in the first place. I don't want to be here now and I'm counting the days until they let me go back to New York," I said.

He grinned. "What makes you so sure you'll want to go rushing back to that rat race?"

I rolled my eyes. "What's there for me here? I'll die of boredom."

He grinned as if he knew a secret joke. I decided right then that I hated him. I had hated him when I was little and he'd made fun of me for being afraid of things, and I still hated him. He hadn't improved one bit. No wonder Dad had gotten out as soon as he could. The only thing I couldn't understand was why in the world Dad had ever wanted to come back!

The big grandfather clock in the hall struck seven.

"Seven o'clock?" I exclaimed. "I'm up at seven o'clock and it's not even a school day?"

"That's late for these parts," Grandpa said. "I'm up at five. So are most folks around here. Need to get the farm chores done early."

The rest of the family arrived in a group at that point. They were all dressed in jeans and sweaters.

"It's freezing down here," Mom said. "It was so warm in bed under that quilt."

"Mine was toasty warm," Katie said.

44

"If you want it warmer down here, someone will have to go chop wood," Grandpa said.

"This is a job for the men," Dad said. "Come on, Beau, let's get going."

They put on their jackets, and pretty soon chopping sounds filtered through the window—chopping sounds and a lot of unprintable exclamations from my dad and hysterical laughter from Beau. I was dying to go out and watch, but I figured my dad might take off one of his feet if I distracted him. So we waited. Mom cooked oatmeal and put out shredded wheat, and Grandpa made some toast. I even drank a cup of coffee to warm me up.

Then the door swung open and Dad and Beau came in, Dad with an armful of logs, Beau with kindling.

Grandpa started to laugh. "It took you all that time and that's all you've got?"

"I'm kind of out of practice," Dad said evenly. "I haven't done this for twenty years, remember? We don't have to chop too much wood in New York. But I started getting the hang of it again."

"I think you did splendidly," Mom said. "Both of you."

"Teach the boy to do it. Build up those spindly arms of his," Grandpa said.

"Yeah, I'm going to do it every day," Beau said proudly. "Then when we go back to New York, I'm going to beat up those kids who took my lunch money."

"We all need to build up our muscles if we're going to be of any use out here," Dad said. "I know

45

that right now I don't have the strength to rope a calf."

"And I've got to get my digging muscles going by the time I want to plant a vegetable garden," Mom said.

I looked from one to the other. They were really looking forward to this. They were actually excited.

"I think I'll go up and finish my letter to Brendan," I said. But when I was upstairs, I found it hard to write. I sat at Dad's old desk, staring out at the mountains, and tried to think of one good thing about being in Wyoming. I wondered how the rest of my family could want this primitive sort of life. *Maybe I was switched at birth,* I decided. *Maybe somewhere in New York there's a civilized, normal family with a daughter who walks around saying* hee-haw!

Suddenly I had to get out of the house. I put on my warmest sweater and leggings and boots and headed downstairs.

"We're all going shopping in Cody, Amber," Katie called. "Want to come?"

The thought of shopping in a nothing town like Cody only depressed me further. "No, thanks," I said. "I'm going for a walk."

I turned onto the road in the opposite direction from the way we had come the night before and headed up the valley. There were golden-green fields on either side of the road, which soon joined the rushing stream. I could hear it babbling and gurgling beside me. The rain that we'd had during the night must have refilled it, because it lapped against the top of its banks. It was the most lonely place I had ever been. There were no houses, no people, no cars, no sounds except for the sigh of wind and the cry of birds—nothing. I'd never been so alone.

I must have gone about a mile when I heard a sound behind me. Over the babble of the stream I heard the swish of long grass and then a snort, which almost made me jump out of my skin. I spun around quickly to see an enormous animal only a few feet away from me, its body still hidden in the grass beside the path. It had huge pointed horns and it was snorting at me in a very unfriendly way. I didn't know much about farms or the countryside, but I had seen movies of bullfights. I knew what bulls did when they didn't like you. Just as I was remembering that, the animal lowered its head, made a low, grunting sound, and started coming toward me.

I didn't wait any longer. I ran as fast as I could along the road. "Help! Help!" I cried.

I don't know whom I expected to hear me in the wilderness. I don't know what I expected to do. I just wanted to reach safety before the bull's horns caught up with me. But there was no safety. A barbed-wire fence now ran on both sides of the road. I kept looking for a gate I could vault over—that was one time I'd have been grateful for my gymnastic training—but no gates appeared. I could hear pounding hoofbeats on the muddy earth behind me as the bull caught up with me. It was giving these weird moans as it came. Any second I expected to be speared by razor-sharp horns.

A picture flashed before my eyes of my parents finding my mangled, trampled body. "If only we hadn't brought her here," they'd say. "If only we'd left her in the safety of New York City."

But I didn't have the time or the energy to think about it, because the bull had caught up with me now. I could feel its hot breath. I had no breath of my own to yell for help anymore.

Then suddenly a miracle occurred. I heard the sound of galloping hooves—a horse approaching fast.

"Help! Over here," I yelled again.

I stumbled and looked up, and felt enormous relief when I saw that it was Rich.

"Help me!" I gasped. "Mad bull. About to be gored."

Instantly he was alert. "The bull's out? Where?"

"Right behind me," I stammered. He had to be either stupid or blind. I could still feel the bull's breath.

"Right behind you?" he said, and he started to laugh. "You mean this here?" He walked his horse up to the brown monster and gave its side a friendly slap. "This here's old Buttercup," he said.

"Old Buttercup?"

"Sure. Wouldn't hurt a fly. My daddy shoulda put her down years ago, but he raised her from a young'un and he always was soft about her. Said she gave him good calves and good milk. So now she's like a pet, just hanging around until someone shows up to make a fuss over her. She can be a pesky nuisance. Followed me to school a couple of times." He moved his horse alongside the cow. "Giddup, girl. Get on home," he said, giving her rump a resounding slap, so that she trotted off in the direction he had come.

48

As this was happening I had time to take in what I had missed before. Behind the fierce head was a cow's body, large udder and all. I flinched in embarrassment.

"There's only one bull you have to worry about around here," he said. "And that's old Barnaby, down in the pasture by the river."

"It was an easy mistake," I said defiantly. "I only saw the head. The rest of it was hidden in the grass. How was I to know?"

Rich looked at me with amusement. "Easy mistake for a city girl," he said. In the bright sunlight I could see him clearly for the first time. Light-brown hair escaping from under the cowboy hat, freckles on his nose, just like mine, and alarmingly blue eyes, which were twinkling. I had to admit he'd grown up from the skinny kid I remembered. He was definitely a hunk. In spite of the cold weather, he was wearing only a long-sleeved T-shirt and jeans, and the T-shirt clung to his muscles like a second skin.

"I'd better be getting back," I said, because I couldn't think of anything else to say and I needed to escape from his mocking grin.

"I expect I'll be seeing a lot of you," Rich said, "since we'll be riding to school together on the bus every morning. Maybe that will give me a chance to teach you the difference between a bull and a cow!"

"Thank you, but I don't intend to sit anywhere near you on a school bus," I said. "I still have this aversion to frogs."

His grin broadened. "Oh, I gave up on frogs years ago," he said. "That's kid stuff."

49

"I'm glad to hear it."

"Now it's rattlesnakes," he said.

"Gee, you farm boys are so full of fun," I said. "I don't know how I'm going to stand the excitement here."

He didn't get my sarcasm. "Yeah, I guess we have to be more exciting than those boring city types," he said. "Are they born wearing dark suits?"

I was getting angrier and more uncomfortable by the second. *Wait until this geek from boonieville gets a taste of a good old New York insult, the crushing New York put-down, and some witty New York sarcasm,* I told myself. *He'll wonder what hit him.*

Unfortunately I was still tired from the day before and my brain must have been numbed by my encounter with the bull—sorry, cow. I couldn't think of one witty comeback.

"Excuse me, your horse is blocking my path," I said frostily. "My parents should be back from the store by now."

He swung his horse around and urged it into an easy lope back up the trail while I walked home with as much dignity as I could muster.

Chapter Six

I T WASN'T FAIR, I decided as I walked. I'd been half blind with panic because I'd thought I was being chased by an angry bull, and there he had sat on his horse, looking down at me and laughing. I wasn't used to being looked down on or laughed at—especially not by a hick cowboy!

Just wait until I get some energy. He's going to be sorry, I promised myself, thinking of all the witty put-downs I could use on him.

As I came up the track to the house I saw that my family had just arrived and were carrying bags of food and supplies into the house.

"How was your walk, honey? See anything interesting?" Mom called.

"Nothing much. A lot of cows," I said, trying to look cool.

"Cows? Will you take me to see them?" Katie

begged. "I want a friendly cow for a pet."

"These don't look too friendly," I said guardedly.

"Maybe they're lonely," she suggested. "Can we go visit?"

"After lunch," Dad grunted, carrying a big load of groceries. "Give us a hand with this stuff, Amber."

"You bought enough to feed an army," I said, picking up one of the bags.

"Well, the cupboard was pretty bare," Mom said, "and it's quite a trip to the store. We didn't want to forget anything."

Grandpa stood there directing us like some general as we staggered past him with bags and boxes.

Lunch was decidedly better than breakfast had been. Mom had bought lots of cold cuts and stuff for a salad and fresh bread.

"I'm going to have to learn to bake my own bread," she said. "The nearest bakery is twenty miles away. We can't drive that far for bread every time we need more."

"You could pick up bread when you drive us to school. That way you wouldn't have to bake," I suggested.

"But I want to bake," she said. "And what's this about driving you to school? There's a bus that picks up all the students."

"Mom, I don't want to ride with a bunch of hicks. It will be frogs down my back all over again . . . and worse."

"You'll have to learn how to handle it, Amber," Mom said. "In any case, we're going to live simply

52

from now on. We'll use the car only when we really have to."

I winced. We'd probably trade the car for a horse and buggy or a couple of mules. Life as I knew it was rapidly evaporating.

"Can we go for a walk and see the cows now?" Katie asked as soon as lunch was over.

"Okay," I said, trying to sound more enthusiastic than I felt.

We walked the same way I had gone that morning. It was late afternoon and the sun was hanging like a red ball over the western mountains. The snow-capped peaks were glowing pink in the twilight.

"It's pretty here. I like it," Katie said. "Do you like it, too?"

"It's pretty," I said, "but I miss my friends. I'm not going to have any friends here. I'm going to hate it."

"I'm going to have friends," Katie said. She skipped ahead of me, chanting, "I'm going to have a cow. I'm going to have a dog. I'm going to have a cat."

A huge bird—an eagle?—was circling overhead. I stopped to admire the lazy way it just glided through the air without moving its wings at all. I'd love to be able to fly like that, just lying in the air and riding the currents. *I'll have to find out what kind of bird it was,* I thought. *I'll need to know stuff like that out here.*

Then I remembered that I was with Katie. She was probably getting bored waiting for me. I looked up, but she was nowhere in sight.

"Katie?" I called as I hurried down the road. "Katie, don't get lost. Wait for me."

"I'm over here, Amber," Katie called. "I've found a friendly cow. Look!"

I followed the direction of her voice and then I stopped, my heart pounding. Katie was halfway across a field, heading toward a big brown bull. There was no mistaking a real bull when I saw one. I took in the massive head, the big, heavy body, the huge horns. What had Rich told me? *There's only one bull around here you have to worry about and he's in a field down by the river.*

"Katie," I said softly, hoping my voice would carry that far. I didn't want to yell in case I startled the bull. She didn't seem to hear me; she was skipping closer by the minute, her hand stretched out in greeting.

There was only one thing I could do. I had to go in there after her. Grandpa had said you had to show animals who was boss, but I didn't think a bull that size would believe me. Every part of me was trembling as I climbed the gate and walked toward Katie. She turned around and saw me. "Hi, Amber, come pet the cow with me!" she said.

"Katie, listen to me," I said in my calmest voice. "I want you to start walking back to me. Don't run. Don't yell. That's a bull and we don't want to upset it. Understand?"

"It might just be lonely," Katie said. "It's got a nice face. I bet it wants a friend."

The bull was now aware of us. He had looked up from his grazing, and he snorted.

I had no alternative. I went all the way up to Katie and I grabbed her hand. "We are getting out of here

54

now," I said. "Just walk away calmly and steadily. If it starts to come after us, then run like crazy for the gate."

This time she didn't argue. She had picked up on my fear. I just hoped the bull hadn't. We started across the field, and I heard the bull snort again. The gate seemed impossibly far away. Then I heard something else—the clip-clop of hoofs as Rich Winter suddenly appeared.

"Oh, my God," he exclaimed. "Don't move. Stand right where you are and don't run."

Then he dismounted, vaulted the gate, and went up to the bull. "Hi there, Barnaby. Hi there, old fella," he said, and he started patting the bull's neck, talking all the time in a low, soothing voice. "Who's a big old softie, eh? Old Barnaby, good old Barnaby."

He looked in our direction. "Now walk to the gate. And whatever you do, don't run," he said.

He stayed with the bull until we were both safely over, then he backed away, talking to the bull all the time until he vaulted over safely himself.

"Thanks," I began, but he turned on me, eyes blazing.

"Are you completely stupid?" he yelled. "Didn't I just tell you this morning that there's only one bull around here you need to worry about? So what do you do? You go visit him! You just don't have a clue, do you? Are all city folk as birdbrained as you? It was a stupid idea for your grandpa to bring you out here. You should have stayed in the city, where you belong."

By that time I was angry as well as scared. "Believe me, it wasn't my idea to come to this backwoods

55

place!" I snapped. "There was nothing I wanted more than to *stay* in the city. And for your information, I am not entirely stupid. My little sister didn't know about the bull, and she was in the middle of that field. Someone had to get her out."

He stared at me. "And you went in there after her?"

"She wouldn't come out by herself," I said, shrugging.

"That was a pretty darned brave thing to do," he said. "Seeing as how you were scared of a harmless cow this morning."

"I didn't have any choice. Is the bull very dangerous?"

"He killed a farmhand once," Rich said. "And he almost took my dad's leg off when he didn't get away fast enough."

"Then you were pretty darned brave to go in there yourself," I said shakily. "Especially to rescue such useless strangers."

We stood there facing each other, his eyes looking steadily into mine. Then he shrugged. "Old Barnaby knows me," he said. "He likes me to scratch him. Just promise me one thing: that you won't go visiting any animals until I educate you on the difference between cows and bulls."

He pushed his hat back on his head and grinned as he picked up his horse's reins.

"I'd like to see you survive in the big city," I called after him. "I'd like to see you cross the street in rush hour and dodge taxis and find the right subway line and not get your wallet stolen. I can do all those things just fine. That's my home territory, where I belong."

I grabbed Katie's hand and started striding for

56

home, dragging her beside me. I heard Rich's foot-steps behind me.

"I'm sorry," he said. "I didn't mean to yell at you just now. I was rattled when I saw you with that bull. I know how fast he can move when he wants to. And you're right about New York City. I wouldn't know how to dodge taxis and muggers."

He squatted down to Katie's height. "You okay now, littl'un? Want a ride?" When she nodded solemnly, he swung her into the saddle. It was strange, but I got the weirdest feeling watching her in his arms, being lifted easily as if she weighed nothing at all. I found myself wondering what it would be like to feel those strong hands around my waist, to brush his face with my hair. Would he have let go of me with a friendly slap, the way he did with Katie? And then I was furious with myself for thinking such dumb things.

"Are you okay up there?" I asked her.

She nodded seriously.

"Just hold on to that horn and you'll be fine," Rich said. He fell into step beside me. "I'll walk you home—just to be on the safe side."

We started walking back along the side of the road. I was so conscious of his closeness that it was hard to get my thoughts in order. I wanted to make light, witty conversation, so that he'd see what sophisticated New Yorkers were like. But I couldn't think of a single thing to say. When a tall stalk of wild rye brushed against my hand, I jumped. For a moment I'd thought it was his hand touching mine.

57

"What now?" he asked with another grin.

"Nothing. Just a bug," I said.

We walked on in silence to the clip-clop of the horse's hoofs. At last Rich broke the silence. "It must have been really tough for you to leave all your friends in the middle of high school."

I nodded. He was being nice to me; I didn't know how to handle it. "You don't know how tough," I said. "I went to this great school that had everything—art, music, drama. I could have gotten into any college I wanted, and now I'm stuck out here."

He digested this. "Yeah, Indian Valley High probably isn't the greatest school in the world," he said. "It's real small, for one thing. But we have a lot of fun—dances and rallies and stuff like that. We've got a combined homecoming and Halloween dance coming up October thirty-first. You want to go?"

I wasn't sure whether he was giving me a general invitation or inviting me as his date. I wasn't sure about the dating rituals of Wyoming people. If I accepted his offer, would I be officially designated as Rich's girl? I could imagine Suzanne's reaction. "I hope you've learned to yell *yahoo* and avoid clodhopper boots," she'd say. I decided to play it safe.

"Uh . . . I don't think so. But thanks," I said. "I left the most wonderful boyfriend in the world at home. I don't think he'd want me going to dances with other guys."

"Just as a friend," Rich said. He sounded hurt. "I was just trying to be friendly, seeing as how you don't know anybody around here. You want to fit in and get to know people and have a good time, don't you?"

"No, I don't," I said. "I didn't want to come here and I can't wait to get back to New York. My dad promised me that he'd let me go back if I'm still unhappy in June. So I intend to be miserable all year."

Rich looked at me strangely. "I'd say that was a dumb way of looking at things," he said. "To my mind you should always try to make the best of any situation."

"And I suppose you think you're the best that Indian Falls has to offer," I snapped, caught off guard by the bluntness of his criticism.

"You said it, not me," he joked, a big grin spreading across his face.

"Come on, Katie, we're almost home now. We can walk the rest of the way," I said, yanking her down from the horse.

"But I like riding," Katie protested as I grabbed her hand.

"Fine, if that's how you want it," Rich said. "There aren't any bulls between here and your gate."

"Thanks again for your help," I mumbled.

"No problem," he said. "That's what we country folk are known for—being simple but helpful!" He made a funny face, and I had to laugh as he swung onto his horse and galloped away. I stood there, staring after him. If he was supposed to be a simple country boy, why was I so unsettled?

Katie tugged at my hand. "I think he likes you, Amber," she said. "Is he going to be your new boyfriend?"

59

"For your information, Katie, I am not going to have any boyfriends while I'm here. I've got Brendan waiting for me at home."

"Then why is your face all red?" Katie demanded.

"I'm hot from all this walking, that's why. Now stop asking stupid questions," I snapped, and walked ahead of her so fast she had to run to catch up.

Chapter Seven

I FELT VERY confused for the rest of the afternoon. Why did Rich Winter make me feel that I was not only a helpless female, but a stupid one too? I was angry at him for showing up and making me look like a fool. I didn't want to think about him and I didn't want to like him. So why couldn't I get him out of my mind?

"Can I call Brendan tonight?" I asked my mother as we cleared the table after dinner. "I need to know that there are still some sane, normal people left in the world."

She smiled and told me not to talk for half the night. That was hardly going to happen, since the only phone in the house was in the unheated front hall, where everyone could hear every word I said. So I tried hard to keep my cool when Brendan's deep, wonderful voice came on the line.

61

"What's up, Amber?" he said in that easy way of his. "Have you learned to say *hee-haw* yet?"

"No, but I've learned the difference between a cow and a bull. And I've learned more about chickens than I'll ever need to know," I said. Then I told him everything. He laughed so hard he started choking. I would have liked him to say, "Gee, you must have been really scared. It would have freaked me out, too," but he didn't.

"I've started writing you a letter," I said shyly.

"Me too. I wrote a whole page during history. You know how boring Mr. Roth is! Oh, and Mandy got your part in the play. She's been dancing around and acting crazy ever since she got it. You know how Mandy gets." Then there was a long pause. "I miss you already," he said softly. "It seems strange without you. I keep expecting you to walk through the door."

"Me too," I said, "only when I walk through the door I see mountains and cows." I glanced back into the living room. "I have to go, Brendan," I said, looking at my watch. "Everyone's listening to our conversation and it's freezing out here. There's only one fireplace in the entire house."

"See, I told you you didn't have anything to worry about," he said.

"What do you mean?"

"You think your parents are going to survive all winter in a freezing house? They'll be fighting each other to get on a plane back to New York, and you'll be back at Dover for the spring semester."

"You really think so?"

62

"I guarantee it," he said in a TV-commercial voice, making me laugh. *Oh, Brendan,* I wanted to say, *I need you here so badly.* But somehow I couldn't make the words come out. It wasn't fair—we'd barely gotten to know each other. We hadn't reached that stage where we were totally comfortable and could say anything to each other. If only I could have stayed in New York just a few weeks more, I might have found out he was the one boy I'd been waiting for all my life. . . .

"Are you still there, Amber?" His voice sounded very distant.

"Yeah. I guess I should go. Bye. Call me soon."

"I will. Bye, Amber. Miss you!" The phone clicked down.

When I hung up, I wasn't sure whether calling him had been a good idea or not. I missed him more than ever and he had sounded so very far away.

That night I lay awake listening to all the strange night noises. There were no familiar city sounds— sirens and car horns and street sweepers—to lull me to sleep. There were only strange cries against the sighing of the wind—owls, or coyotes maybe—that reminded me I was very, very far from home.

Monday morning was my first day at the new school. I woke up with a tight knot in my stomach, and began to wish I were anywhere else in the world. It was almost the end of October, so the rest of the kids at Indian Valley High had been in school for two months and were already familiar with their classes, their teachers, and each other. I was never going to fit in, even if I wanted to. Which I didn't.

I took a lot of trouble with the way I looked. It was important for those hicks to know that they were dealing with someone who wore very cool clothes and was more sophisticated than they could ever hope to be. I must have tried on every outfit I had, but in the end I chose my favorite baggy overalls with the holes in both knees, an oversized plaid flannel shirt with a hood, and a vest to go over it. The vest, which was covered with buttons and little patches of strange fabrics, was one of a kind; I'd bought it at an art show in Central Park. I grinned when I saw my reflection in the mirror. *Wait until these hicks see me!* I thought. I used my curling iron to make long, spiral curls in my hair and spent lots of time on my makeup. When I'd finished I looked exactly the way I liked: enough pale foundation to hide the freckles, and very dark plum lips. Totally artsy! I loved it.

My mother drove me to register at Indian Valley High. At first glance it looked modern enough. I'd expected a one-room schoolhouse, but it was all concrete and glass, with a huge football field on one side.

I hated the principal, Mr. Houghton, at first sight. He was big and red and jolly and he called me "little lady." We spent an exciting hour with him while we tried to arrive at a schedule that would give me some of the classes I wanted. It seemed that sophomores there usually took geometry, but I was already taking intermediate algebra. Mr. Houghton looked really worried about putting me in with a class of juniors. He also looked worried about putting

64

me in biology, because the class was so crowded. He suggested home ec instead. Mom kept glancing nervously across at me, answering for me before I totally lost my cool and told Mr. Houghton what I thought of him and his school.

By the end of the hour, I had confirmed all my worst suspicions. No drama, no music except a stupid marching band, and no advanced art. I had a schedule that was boring, boring, boring.

"Bye, honey. Have a great first day," Mom said, kissing my cheek.

"Bye," I said, my face letting her know exactly what I thought of that first day. "I'm sure I'll have a ball."

By lunchtime I felt like an alien from another planet. Everyone noticed me instantly and asked where I came from. When I told them New York City, they asked the most ridiculous questions.

"Did you ever get shot at?"

"Did everyone in your old school carry guns and knives?"

"Did you get mugged very often?"

Then they all wanted to know what I was doing there. It seemed simpler to say that we'd come to look after my grandfather than to explain the other reasons.

"So tell me, Amber," one of the girls said (her name was Mary Beth, I think—I was a little confused, because there was also a Mary Jo and a Mary Ann). "Does everyone in New York City dress like you?"

"Well, not exactly," I said. "The people who go to work usually wear suits. People from the Village dress like me. They find all kinds of great stuff in thrift shops and then update it. I've even got clothes from the seventies."

They nodded, wide-eyed and polite, taking it all in.

"I guess it must be a relief to be here, where nobody cares how you dress," one of them said. "I had to wear the same pair of jeans for a month once. I hated it."

I wasn't quite sure what she was getting at, but I smiled politely.

"I bet you're glad to be here, where folks are friendly and it's safe to go out, aren't you?" I got asked over and over.

I was very tempted to tell them exactly what I thought about being in Wyoming. I hadn't intended to make friends with anyone. I was determined to hate it there. But for the first time in my life I was the center of attention. Also, I couldn't help remembering what Rich had said about trying to make the best of a situation. So I swallowed my words and managed a smile. I looked up to see Rich crossing the lunchroom toward me.

"Hey," he said. "How are you surviving so far?"

"I'm still here," I said, spreading my hands and blushing.

"Yeah, I reckon you're safe enough here," he said. "They've got gates around the school to keep out the wild animals."

"I don't know about that," I countered. "I've met plenty of wolves and bores already!"

His face creased into a smile. "And I reckon you know how to handle them, too," he acknowledged.

66

"Well, I'd better be going. Just wanted to check on you. See ya on the bus tonight, then."

He turned to my group of admirers. "Be nice to her, okay? She's still in culture shock."

Then he strolled away.

"Boy, you don't waste any time, do you?" Mary Beth exclaimed. "Rich Winter! He's the biggest hunk in the school."

"He's only being nice because he's my next-door neighbor," I said, trying to sound cool. "I have a really cute boyfriend back in New York."

"I'd say New York was an awful long way from here," one of the other girls said speculatively. "I don't care how cute the boyfriend is, you wouldn't catch me looking the other way if Rich Winter were interested in me."

I found my eyes following Rich across the lunchroom. *Don't be stupid,* I told to myself. I was not so desperate that I was going to latch on to the first hick cowboy who took an interest in me. Even if he did have gorgeous blue eyes and great muscles. Rich was just being friendly and I was really, truly not interested.

"So how did it go?" Rich asked me later as we boarded the school bus to go home. "Nice bunch of kids, huh? Real friendly."

"Very friendly," I agreed. They *had* been friendly enough. It was just that they were from nowhereville. I'd listened in on conversations and hadn't had a clue what they were talking about. They'd asked me what music I liked, but they'd never heard of my favorite groups. I'd tried to tell them about movies I had seen, but except for ones starring Bruce Willis or Julia Roberts, they'd never heard of them. And as for clothes . . . well, they certainly needed some help with their wardrobes. There were jeans and flannel shirts, only they all looked brand-new—no old Levi's 501s here. Some of the girls wore plain shirts and some of them even wore pleated skirts. Everybody looked very neat and tidy—and exactly the same. No rips, no baggies, no ultra-mini skirts, no leather, nothing fun or unusual or artistic. And they'd looked at my clothes as if they'd never seen anything like them before.

"One girl asked me if I knew that the knees of my overalls were ripped," I said to Rich, thinking it was very funny.

"That was rude of her," he commented. "Who was it?"

"I don't know her name. I just thought it was kind of funny," I said.

He didn't smile.

I arrived home to find Beau and Katie already at the kitchen table, eating bread and peanut butter.

I took a plate. "Pass the bread, please."

"Are you sure?" Beau asked.

"What's wrong with it?"

"Mom baked it."

"It looks okay."

"Go ahead. Try it," Beau said, pushing the bread in my direction.

I spread it liberally with peanut butter and took a bite. It was like biting into a rock. I felt my jaw snap back as I tried to chew.

"Kind of hard, right?" Katie asked. "I nearly lost my wiggly tooth and then Mom would have had to give me a dollar."

"Don't try to swallow it—you'll choke. You'll die a horrible death," Beau warned. "You have to soak it in milk forever before you can eat it."

At that moment Mom appeared. "So, how's the bread?" she asked with a big, hopeful smile on her face.

"It's . . . uh . . . great," we all said.

"I know it's not perfect yet, but it's my first attempt," she said. "I'm glad it went so well. I think I'm getting the hang of this country-living stuff already."

She swept out again and we all just looked at each other, trying to decide how to handle this. Grandpa came in, took a slice, spread jelly on it, and then took a big bite. We watched in silence.

"Holy Moses, what is this supposed to be?" he demanded.

"Mom's first attempt at baking," I told him.

"I nearly lost the rest of my teeth!"

"Me too, Grandpa," Katie said. "My tooth is more wiggly now. See?"

"Want me to pull it out for you?" he asked.

"No, it might hurt."

"Nah. It'll be over in a second. I always pulled your dad's teeth out. Then you can put it under your pillow and get a dime."

"A dime? Grandpa, I get a dollar!"

"A whole dollar for a tooth! That's highway robbery," he said. "For that kind of money, I might just eat more of that bread and make my own teeth fall out!"

Katie giggled.

Mom came into the kitchen again. "Oh, Pa, you're eating my first attempt at breadmaking. How is it?"

"I've tasted worse," he said, winking in our direction. As we heard my mother's heels clatter down the front steps he whispered, "It will come in handy when we need to throw something to get the crows off the crops!"

We all burst out laughing, and I began to wonder if he was really so bad after all.

I'd just finished my homework when I heard the sound of a car coming up the driveway. I looked out in time to see a battered old truck stop outside and Rich get out. Immediately my heart started racing. Rich had come to visit me. Why? I wondered. Maybe he wanted to do homework together, just like Brendan and I had started to do. Or maybe he just wanted to hang out. I could play him all my newest CDs. . . . I thought about how cool it would be to let all my new friends know about this visit.

I heard voices in the hallway and then Mom called, "Amber, you've got a visitor."

I came downstairs. Rich was standing in the front hall with a big cardboard box in his hands. "I brought this for you," he said.

"What is it?" I asked, mystified. I was even more mystified when I opened it and the first thing I saw was a pair of jeans.

Rich looked embarrassed. "Some of the kids at school today felt sorry that you didn't have anything better to wear on your first day than those ripped old overalls. So we took up a collection among us and we've got a couple of pairs of jeans that aren't ripped and some decent shirts too."

"You what?" I stammered.

He went on smoothly, not sensing that I was about to lose control. "The girls were upset that you had to wear those ripped overalls and that your vest was held together with patches and old buttons. I hope you don't mind taking charity like this. It's meant with the best intentions."

"For your information," I said icily, "the outfit I'm wearing today cost a fortune."

"It did?"

"Sure. Everything came from the most trendy boutiques in the Village. That's the way hip people dress in the city. It's called fashion in New York."

He looked at me as if he wasn't sure whether I was putting him on or not. "Clothes with holes in them? That's fashionable?" He hesitated and then said, "Look, Amber, it's okay, you don't have to pretend with me. We heard about your dad losing all his money and bringing you guys back here."

The anger I was trying to restrain finally exploded. "Lost his money? My dad is a big-time lawyer. We had an apartment overlooking Central Park! We only came back here to look after my dumb grandfather. We have plenty of money. I think I paid over fifty dollars for these overalls."

"Fifty dollars! Holy cow—you got ripped off! Out here you can buy a perfectly good pair with no holes in the knees for twenty."

I didn't know whether to laugh or cry. How could he be so stupid? Didn't these people read magazines, watch TV? My face was hot with embarrassment. Rich hadn't wanted to hang out with me—he'd felt sorry for me! Nobody had ever felt sorry for me before, and I hated it. "You don't understand, do you?" I demanded. "But how could you, stuck out here in the boonies? You probably buy all your clothes from catalogues. Please take this stuff back and say thanks, but no thanks. I really do have enough clothes—a whole closetful, in fact." I was almost crying by this time. "Would you please go?" I begged.

"Sure," he said. "I didn't mean to upset you."

"Well, you did. You insulted me. It just confirms what I already knew—that I don't belong here."

He picked up the box. "We were only trying to be friendly," he said. "Only trying to make you feel welcome."

"I don't want to make friends here," I snapped. "I want to go back where I belong."

"Suit yourself," he said as he stomped off into the night.

My mother stopped me as I fled up the stairs. "It was nice of Rich to stop by."

"Oh, sure, it was great," I said. "I enjoyed every minute of it. He brought me clothes, Mother. The kids at school all felt sorry for me because my overalls have holes in them. It's not funny," I added as she started to laugh.

"I'm sorry, honey, but it really is funny," she said. "And you did ask for it, dressing in your wildest clothes for the first day. They're very conservative here, you know. They probably don't understand about Greenwich Village fashion."

"Which proves my point exactly," I said. "I told you I don't belong here. I told you I'd hate it. Now do you see what you're putting me through? I can't go back to that school and face those kids again. I'll be a laughingstock."

"Of course you won't. I think it's sweet that they were trying to be nice. All you have to do is pick out some less flamboyant clothes until you settle in."

"I don't want to settle in!" I shouted. "I want to go home!"

Chapter Eight

M Y PARENTS PRACTICALLY had to drag me to the school bus the next morning. I didn't know how I was going to face any of those ignorant hicks. And more important, I didn't know how I was going to face Rich. He was sure to have told everyone about the scene I made last night by then. They'd all be whispering behind my back and snickering as I walked past them. It was only after my father threatened to carry me into the classroom over his shoulder that I agreed to go.

I was determined to make sure that nobody ever again thought I was poor. I put on my raw-silk pants, my imported English cashmere sweater, and my black leather jacket. They'd see that I could dress like a million bucks if I wanted to.

Rich's eyes opened with surprise when I got on the bus. I gave him my most hostile, defiant stare as I swept past him. He flushed and pretended to be busy with a textbook. As soon as I sat down I felt bad about the way I'd yelled at him the night before. After all, he'd only been the messenger. He was just trying to help. It wasn't his fault that we were people from two different worlds with absolutely nothing in common. But I didn't know what to say to make things better. So I sat in silence all the way to school.

At lunchtime the group of girls I'd hung around with the day before came up to me, looking very apologetic. "We're sorry about what happened last night. We only wanted to help," Mary Beth said. "We didn't mean to offend you, Amber."

"It's okay," I managed to say graciously. "How were you to know?" I was about to add something about living in the boonies, but I bit my tongue at the last second.

"So you forgive us?" Mary Jo asked. "We don't want you to be mad at us. Maybe you can tell us about New York fashion. It would be kind of fun."

They were trying their hardest. I managed a smile.

"Are you coming to cheerleading practice after school?" Mary Jo asked.

I was about to say that I thought cheerleading was one of the world's most stupid activities when she added, "I don't know if anybody has told you, but Tuesday, Wednesday, and Thursday we don't have seventh-period classes. The boys have football practice instead. That way they can still catch the school bus home."

"They shorten school for football?" I said in amazement.

"Yes. And cheerleading. Or if you don't want to do that, you can go to the library and get your homework done. Or you can watch the guys."

"You mean there are no sports activities for girls?"

"Well, not right now," she said. "In the winter we get to play basketball, when the guys don't need the court. And in the spring we can run track."

"Big deal," I said angrily. "Isn't it illegal not to offer the same programs for girls and guys?"

Mary Beth laughed. "Don't be silly, Amber. Girls can't play football," she said. "Besides, we don't mind. I like getting my homework finished early. Gives me time for my chores."

I could see I wasn't about to convert her in a hurry, but I decided to mention it to my father, the lawyer. I was sure it was illegal to offer no sports for girls when all that time and money was spent on guys. For a second I visualized myself updating the school single-handedly. We'd have volleyball and girls' tennis and maybe even gymnastics. Then I remembered that I didn't care one way or the other. What did it matter what happened at Indian Valley High? I was going back to New York the next year.

So Mary Beth went to do homework in the library, but I decided to go along with bouncy Mary Jo to cheerleading practice. I'd never been at a school with cheerleaders before and I was kind of curious. Besides, I'd been sitting in stuffy rooms all day. It'd be nice to do something physical.

"It's kind of fun and it's not hard," Mary Jo confided as she walked beside me. "Most of the girls

76

aren't very good, so we do real simple moves. Everyone who tries out makes it. I'm sure you'll be able to pick it up okay if you want to join."

My first look at the Indian Valley High cheerleaders told me that she was certainly right. They didn't have a clue. Kicks with bent knees, pompoms waved every which way. After they had finished a cheer, Mary Jo introduced me to everyone. The school was so small, most of them already knew who I was.

"So are you going to teach us any fancy New York cheers?" a big redheaded girl asked me defiantly.

"I've never been a cheerleader before," I said. "My school didn't have a football team."

"Didn't have a football team? What kind of school was that?" They looked at me with pity, as if I'd been to a school for freaks and weirdos.

"We had too much other stuff," I said. "Great theater and dance and art."

I noticed a bunch of them sniggering behind their hands. They thought I went to a wimpo school.

"You're welcome to watch today and see if you can pick up the routines we do," another girl said kindly. She was the tall blond girl Mary Beth had pointed out as the student-council secretary. "Although it is kind of late in the season now. We've all been working together since August, and if you haven't had any experience . . ."

"I'll give it a try," I said. "I'm a quick learner."

I sat politely and watched. After a while something struck me. "You don't do any tumbling routines or pyramids?"

"We do cartwheels," offered another girl.

77

I couldn't resist it any longer. "But nothing like this?" I asked sweetly. I walked out onto the floor and did back handsprings across the whole length of the floor. When I'd finished, there was total silence.

"Where did you learn that?" someone asked at last.

"I took gymnastics for years."

"Wow! Are you going to the Olympics or something?"

"I'm not good enough for that," I said. "And I grew too tall. That's why I stopped. But I did get to the highest level."

"Do that again," Mary Jo said excitedly.

I demonstrated.

"Do you think you could teach us something like that?" They were crowding around excitedly.

"I could teach you all some basic tumbling stunts," I said. "It would make your routines more fun."

"It sure would," Becky said. "Do something else."

I did all the things I could remember—flip-flops and walkovers and no-handed cartwheels and a couple of aerials. They were very impressed.

"Just wait till those football guys see this! They think they're so hot!" Mary Jo shrieked.

I looked from one face to the next. I had only meant to demonstrate that I wasn't the wimp they thought I was and that New York City was better than Wyoming. I hadn't meant to start a whole feminist movement at Indian Valley High, but it looked as if that was exactly what I had done.

"Maybe Amber could teach us a routine for the homecoming game on Saturday," Becky suggested. "I

78

know we could never learn what she does by then, but we could do enough to surprise people. Make them sit up and notice us."

They crowded around me. "Yeah, let's do it. What do you say, Amber?" they asked. "Could you teach us some of those things? Maybe there are some easy stunts that look real impressive?"

They were so excited, they wanted to start working right away. I had to remember back to my first tumbling classes, and I got them all doing handstands against the wall. One thing was clear—they all had good muscles from those farm chores. By the end of the afternoon they had mastered several basic stunts, so I got them started on a pyramid. It was pretty basic, and I topped it by climbing onto a big, beefy girl's shoulders.

"Ta-da!" one of the onlookers shrieked, and everyone applauded. I looked up to find that some of the football team had silently come in and that Rich was standing a few feet away, watching us. I don't know why that threw me. I'd had plenty of people watch me before. And maybe the other girls got nervous at the same time, noticing that the football players were there. All I know is that suddenly it seemed as if Alison's shoulders were shaking like an earthquake, and then I lost my balance.

"Whoa!" I yelled as I felt myself falling. But suddenly strong arms were around me.

"Don't worry, I've got you," Rich said. His face was looking worriedly into mine, and I was all too conscious of his warmth and closeness and the strength of his arms holding me.

"Thanks," I muttered, "but you didn't have to worry. We gymnasts know how to fall properly."

"Sorry," he said, his expression uneasy. "All I saw was you and the floor about to meet each other."

I remembered how I'd yelled at him the night before. I couldn't make him feel bad again. "How were you to know?" I said. "Thanks for the thought."

His eyes smiled at me. "That was pretty impressive stuff. I didn't know you'd worked for a circus in New York," he said as he lowered me to the ground.

"Yep," I said, smiling back at him. "Wild-animal trainer."

His grin spread. "Look, I'm sorry I got you all upset last night. I really had no idea. Heck, what do we know about how things are done in New York? No offense meant."

"None taken," I replied. I was very conscious that his hand was still on my arm.

The rest of the pyramid was being helped up and some of the football guys were laughing stupidly. "Some pyramid! Yeah, real impressive, girls. Just don't embarrass us by trying it at halftime."

"You'd better watch out, Chuck Harris," Becky said smoothly. "We might embarrass you by making your football game look less exciting than the halftime show."

"Yeah, sure," the boys said, strolling off.

"We'll show them," Mary Jo muttered.

I turned to see Rich walking out. He looked back, and I gave him my best smile. He gave me the most wonderful smile in return.

"I can't believe the way Rich caught you," Becky

said admiringly. "You ought to put that in the program."

"Are you crazy?" I said. "He might drop me next time!"

They linked arms with me as we walked back to the girls' locker room.

"I'm so excited," Becky said. "I can't wait until we do our halftime show."

"It's going to be the best show there ever was. We might even win the state cheerleading championships now that we've got Amber."

They were loud and excited, already changed from the sweet, uncertain girls I'd met an hour before. I found myself caught up in their excitement. I imagined all the great routines I'd teach them. And then holding the cup we'd win at the state championship. I'd be the heroine of the school.

Wait a minute, I told myself, snapping back to reality. *You don't want to get involved here. You don't want to have fun. You want to go home.*

I remembered what Brendan had said about my parents giving up and going home by the end of the year. Between Mom's baking and my dad's tense relationship with Grandpa, that might well turn out to be true. It had been my one secret hope, but suddenly I found myself thinking that the end of the year would be too soon. The state championships weren't until February.

We worked hard all week, both at lunchtime and during seventh period, practicing like crazy. I had to admire their enthusiasm. Back home it wasn't cool to show enthusiasm. Everything was a big bore. And you had to turn up late. These kids bubbled with enthusiasm, like actors in chewing-gum commercials. And they weren't quitters, either. They fell and collapsed and looked stupid, then they got right up and tried again. And even though I told myself that the halftime show was no big deal for a person like myself, I got caught up in their excitement. I *wanted* them to succeed.

By the end of the week I had taught them a few moves that looked impressive but were really very simple. And I'd found a uniform that fit. I stood in front of the mirror at Grandpa's, looking at myself. Amber Stevens—a cheerleader, complete with pompoms in my hands. I decided I looked pretty good, until I thought of Brendan and Suzanne. They would have died laughing if they could have seen me.

I didn't mention cheerleading when I finished my next letter to Brendan. I didn't mention Rich, either, even though I had sat with him on the bus home for the past two afternoons. I kept telling myself that there was nothing more to this than a friendly guy being nice to a newcomer. I was allowed to have guys as friends, wasn't I? Once I'd thought about it, I knew I didn't really want to spend a whole year being miserable. I just wanted my parents to *think* that I was suffering so they'd send me back home. Of course I wanted to go back to New York and Dover Prep. Back to Brendan and Suzanne. But hanging out with Rich wouldn't be the worst way to spend a year.

Rich was a simple country boy. He'd never be Brendan. He'd never be able to make clever remarks like Brendan, or make me laugh like Brendan, or make me feel like I was on fire when he kissed me, like Brendan. Then I wondered just what it would be like if Rich ever did take me in those strong, muscular arms, his lips moving toward mine and . . . *Stop it!* I yelled to my imagination. Brendan was special and wonderful and *he* was my guy. *Brendan Cooper,* I wrote all around the edges of my binder. My Brendan Cooper.

It was weird that I had been thinking of him, because when I walked in the door on Thursday afternoon, the phone rang and it was Brendan himself. This time there was nobody else listening.

"We just got back from Fiorelli's," he said, "and I had to hear your voice. We were planning a Halloween party, and I suddenly felt so bad that you weren't going to be there. We were coming up with such great costume ideas. I thought of going as Aladdin, but I don't have my princess. I thought of going as pepper, but I need my salt. I thought of going as a centipede, but I don't have enough legs alone. I'll never win the prize without you. Suzanne is going to be Cleopatra. She'll look great!" His wonderful laugh floated through the chilly air of our front hall. I closed my eyes, trying to picture him right there beside me.

"Are your folks starting to crack yet?" he asked, still laughing. "Have they been gored by mad sheep or trampled in a stampede? Frozen to death, maybe?"

"Not even close. They actually like living out here," I said.

"Don't worry, it will happen soon. Remember, I guarantee it!"

I stared at the phone long after he had hung up. I

was glad he'd called, because it reminded me how funny he really was. "I really miss him," I told myself. It was okay to have a friend like Rich to hang out with while I was in Wyoming, but he'd never be in Brendan's league. It was only afterward that I realized I hadn't told him anything about homecoming. That really would have given him something to laugh about.

The homecoming game was Saturday afternoon, which also happened to be Halloween. There would be a parade first and a nighttime dance at school, the one I'd told Rich I wasn't going to. He hadn't brought it up again, and I'd put it out of my head until Mary Beth asked, "You did hear about the dance, didn't you? Tell me you're going to go."

"I don't think so," I said. "I already told Rich that I wasn't going."

"Rich Winter asked you to the dance?" Mary Jo asked in amazement. "And you turned him down?"

"I didn't think my boyfriend in New York would like me going to a dance with another guy," I said slowly, trying to forget Brendan's phone call.

"You wouldn't catch me turning down an invitation from Rich Winter," Mary Beth said. "He'd only have to snap his fingers in my direction and I'd come running."

"He doesn't have a girlfriend?" I asked casually.

"He hasn't dated anyone since Emily, has he?" Mary Beth asked Mary Jo.

They looked at each other.

"What happened to Emily?" I asked.

"Her family moved away. He took it real hard," Mary Jo confided.

I nodded, digesting the information. I was amazed at the surge of excitement I'd felt when I heard he didn't have a girlfriend. I also began to feel bad that I'd turned Rich down. Maybe I had hurt his feelings. But it was too late to go back on that. I could hardly say, "I've decided to go after all." And anyway, I didn't want my parents to see me going to a dance after my first week of school.

"You see," they'd say triumphantly. "You are having a good time here after all."

I had no plans to tell them about the homecoming game, either, but they caught me coming downstairs on Saturday morning wearing my cheerleading outfit, my hair in a neat ponytail.

"Well, well," my father said, giving my mother a wink. "Who would ever have thought it?"

"It's only because there are no sports for girls at this crummy school," I said defensively. "And I don't want to get completely out of shape, so I'm coaching the cheerleading team."

"Do you have a game today?"

"It's homecoming—a big day around here. We have the parade first and then the game." I didn't mention the dance in the evening.

"Why didn't you tell us before, Amber?" my mother said. "We have to come and watch the parade."

"Mom, I'm sure it's totally pathetic," I said.

"I want to watch the parade," Katie said.

85

"It won't be anything like the Macy's parade, you know," I said. "It will be lame."

"It's good to get the feel of a community," my father said. "We'll drive you to school and then we'll watch."

"It's okay. I'm getting a ride with Rich in his truck, so you don't have to worry about driving me."

My father turned to Grandpa. "Do you feel like coming along, too, Dad? Or do you think it will be too much for you?"

"I'd like to come, if there's room," Grandpa said. "I haven't been to a parade in years. I still remember when we went to watch you."

"Were you on the football team, Dad?" I asked.

He shook his head. "I was never tough enough for football. Besides, those guys were all brainless idiots. They used to butt heads for fun. I played the drums in the band."

"You played the drums? I never knew that," I said.

Dad grinned. "There's a lot about my past you don't know. I might rediscover old girlfriends at the parade today."

"This I have to see," Mom said, giving him a friendly push. I noticed that they both looked relaxed. The frown lines on their foreheads were beginning to soften, and they were smiling on a regular basis. Then Mom slapped her hand on the kitchen table. "Oh, no," she said. "I was planning to bake this morning. Now we won't have any bread for tomorrow."

"That's okay," we all said in unison.

She looked from one face to the next. "That bad, huh?" she asked.

"Don't fret about it, Sylvia," Grandpa said. "Jake's mother nearly killed me with her baking when we were first married, but she wound up taking first prize at the fair. All you need is a little practice."

Mom went over and gave him a peck on the cheek. "Thanks, Pa," she said.

A horn sounded in the driveway.

"That's Rich. I've gotta go," I said.

I heard my father say, "What did I tell you?"

I turned back with what I hoped was a frosty expression on my face. "Just because I'm riding to school with Rich doesn't mean anything except that I'd rather not walk five miles. Rich happens to be our nearest neighbor with a truck, and he has to be at school at the same time as me. Okay?"

"Okay, honey, keep your hair on," my father said, still looking amused. "Nobody suggested anything else. We'll see you later. Have a good time."

My face was crimson as I ran outside.

"What's the matter with you?" Rich asked, leaning across to open the door for me.

"Dumb parents," I muttered. "They always read too much into the simplest little thing."

"Like?"

"Like your giving me a ride to the game."

"I know what you mean," he said, grinning at my discomfort. "My folks are exactly the same. My pa was teasing the heck out of me about going after a New York girl."

"He was?"

"Yeah. But I set him straight. I told him I'd be wasting my time, seeing as how you've already got a boyfriend and you can't wait to get back there."

"That's right," I said, staring straight ahead.

Chapter Nine

THE PARADE WAS certainly corny, and very, very small. Anyone who'd ever been at the Macy's Thanksgiving Day Parade would have laughed themselves silly. But these people seemed to think it was pretty good! We started off at the football field, with a fire truck and police car leading the way. Then came the band, and an open truck with the football team in it. We cheerleaders walked behind, waving pompoms, followed by floats for each of the classes. The last truck carried the queen and her princesses. We walked down the road as far as the public-services building, around the park, and back again. That was about it. Everyone called out to us as we went past:

"Don't drop those pompoms, Mary Jo!"

"You yell nice and loud, Becky!"

"Lookin' real pretty today, Laurie Beth."

Sometimes the comments weren't so polite. Mary Jo, walking beside me, made a face.

"Just because he's my cousin, he thinks he can say stuff like that," she huffed.

The football game was against the Cody Tigers. It was close and exciting, with a lot of cheering from the bleachers. I'd never been to a football game before; everything happened so quickly, it wasn't always possible to tell what was going on. I just kept my eyes on Rich, number eighty-four. I watched him do some pretty spectacular runs down the field. And once the quarterback lobbed a long pass as Rich flew down the sideline, making a diving catch and scattering us cheerleaders as he slid out of bounds. For a moment I was worried and almost ran to see if he was okay. But then he scrambled to his feet amidst wild cheers.

"A gain of thirty yards on the play," the announcer boomed. "A fine catch from number eighty-four, Rich Winter." And I found I was feeling as proud as if it had been me.

Then came halftime and we walked out to do our show. As our music blared over the loudspeakers my knees actually trembled. It had to be from the cold. I had never felt nervous when I performed at Dover—and important people had been in the audience. But maybe that was because I'd always been in the background before, and had never been the star. It had never really mattered whether I messed up or not. This time I knew that all these girls were relying on me.

The music started. The rest of the girls ran out in a

line, pompoms above their heads. Then I ran out and did back handsprings all the way past them, picking up my pompoms as I landed on the last flip. I heard a collective gasp and then everyone went wild. I couldn't believe the crowd could make so much noise. They loved everything we did. They screamed and yelled, and when we finished with the pyramid they gave us a standing ovation. The girls went crazy with excitement as we ran off the field.

"Did you hear that? They loved it! We're a hit! We're famous!" We were hugging and jumping around, and I was right in the middle of it.

"Amber, you did it!" Becky said, squeezing my arm.

"We all did it. You guys managed to learn all that stuff in less than a week."

"But we never could have done it without you," Mary Jo said. "I'm so glad you came to our school. I bet we really could have a shot at the state championship this year."

We went back for the second half of the game and won by a field goal. Rich passed me as we headed off the field.

"Hey, Amber, put it there!" he yelled, and high-fived me.

"You were great out there," I said, lightly slapping his hand.

"And you weren't so bad yourself," he said. "Some fancy tumbling, I'd say!"

We just stood there with the crowd surging around us.

"Okay, so we were both pretty good," I agreed.

"See, we do have something in common after all," he said. "We're both brilliant!"

"And equally humble," I said with a laugh as the crowd began to separate us.

He looked back as he was swept forward by the tide. "Hey, Amber," he yelled, but I couldn't hear the rest of what he said.

It was hard even to make it to the locker room. People I didn't know kept thumping me on the back and telling me how great the show had been.

I had a big smile on my face as I headed for the door, and was surprised when one of the football players grabbed my arm. "Yo, new girl," he said. "Did you hear about the party tonight? Some of us are planning a special Halloween party before the dance. We're going to meet at the old Samson place at seven. It's that house with the big trees, just before you get to the gas station. Nobody lives there now, so it's great for a Halloween party. Hope you can come."

"Sure. Do I have to bring anything?"

"Oh, no. Just yourself," he said. "Make sure you wear a costume, of course. And don't go blabbing all over school about it. It's just the team and a few special friends getting together." He gave me a knowing wink before he turned to go.

I walked on with an amazed smile on my face. I'd been in the place a week and already I was part of the select group—the football stars and the cheerleaders. I suppose it was only natural that it should go to my head a little. From being a background sort of person at Dover, I was now Miss Hotshot Celebrity, and it wasn't all bad. And something else occurred to me, too. If the party was football guys and their friends, then Rich would be there and it would be very natural if a whole group of us went on to the dance afterward. . . .

My family made a huge fuss over me when I got home. You'd have thought I'd just won an Olympic medal or something. I was pretty sure part of the reason was that they were trying to send out positive vibes to me and make me realize how valuable I was there. Still, it felt good. I couldn't think of a time in my life when my family had treated me like a hero before.

"You were the best one, Amber," Katie said, hugging me.

"Don't go on at her," Grandpa growled. "You're giving her a swelled head. I'll need to enlarge the doorway to let her in."

"But she was the best, wasn't she?" Beau insisted. "You said she was amazing. I heard you."

"Hmph," Grandpa said, pretending to be busy poking the fire. "Anyone would think I've got myself a circus for a family, what with Amber flying through the air like that. Now I'm going to go sit down and read. Too much standing for one day. Those football games go on forever." Then he stomped off, his crutches clomping on the floor. My parents looked at each other and grinned.

"He was very impressed, Amber," my dad whispered. "He kept telling everyone you're his granddaughter. Now he's embarrassed about it."

We continued to talk about the game and the parade all through dinner. I don't know who had more fun that day—my family or me.

"I have to go get ready," I said after we'd finished eating. "I've been invited to a very select Halloween party this evening. I have to invent a costume."

"You could be a witch, like me," Katie suggested.

"I don't have time to make a witch's costume," I said. "I'll go upstairs and see what inspiration I can get."

I looked through my closet and decided I'd have to go as a hippie. Like I said, I already had a lot of seventies stuff. I decided on my bell-bottoms and a tie-dyed T-shirt. I braided my hair, wore a headband, and painted a peace symbol on my forehead. I thought I looked pretty cool when I set off for the Samson house, Grandpa's directions in my hand. I passed a pint-sized pirate and a ghost, out trick-or-treating with no adult in attendance. There were jack-o'-lanterns outside front doors. Trees creaked and swayed in the wind. It was my first real spooky Halloween, and I liked the feeling of being out in the cold and dark alone.

The rickety old gate to the Samson place was half open. Through the darkness I could just make out the shape of the big old house ahead. There were no lights in the windows, and I wondered if they'd managed to black them out for better effect. *They know how to do things in Wyoming after all,* I thought. *My friends wouldn't have gone to all this trouble back in New York.*

I looked around, expecting to see other people arriving, but the path to the house was black and deserted. Big old trees creaked and groaned as I walked

94

along. Before I got to the house the path crossed a little stream by a rickety old bridge, and then went up some steps to the front door. I stood on the front porch, waiting and listening for sounds of life. But there was no laughter or music. Nothing. *I must be early*, I thought. *Maybe they're still setting up in a back room.*

Hesitantly I knocked on the front door. "Hello," I called. "Is anyone there?"

The front door creaked spookily open, revealing an expanse of blackness. "Hi," I called. "Are you guys in there?"

I thought I saw a glimmer of light off to my left. I was right. They were in a back room. They probably had music on and couldn't hear the front door. I crossed the front hall and started down a side passage. Suddenly there was a flash of light, like car headlights turning onto the main road. And then right in front of me was this . . . thing. It was hovering in the doorway, all white and misty-looking. It moaned and started to billow out toward me.

"Aaah!" I screamed, stumbling backward.

I put out my hand in the total darkness, expecting to find a wall. Instead I touched a sticky, clingy cobweb. Turning around, I ran out of that house as fast as I could. Stumbling down the steps, I looked back. The shape still seemed to be behind me. I flew down the path to the bridge and was halfway across when suddenly there was no more bridge. I screamed again, then gasped as I plunged down, landing up to my knees in icy water.

A great roar of laughter went up and flashlights

clicked on. They were pointing at me, standing there terrified and helpless in the stream.

"Hey, New York girl, welcome to Wyoming," a male voice roared.

"Aren't you going to fly out of the water? How about a couple of somersaults now?"

More dumb laughter. I recognized the faces of guys on the football team, looking creepy in the uneven light. I hauled myself from the freezing water with as much dignity as I could muster. It wasn't easy in waterlogged bell-bottoms that suddenly weighed a ton and cork-soled platform shoes that squelched as I walked.

"I'll tell you the difference between guys in New York and guys here," I said haughtily. "In New York they've grown up by the time they're high-school seniors. They're already men, not pathetic little boys like you. No wonder you have to spend Halloween like this! It's because no girls would want to date immature idiots like you. Now get out of my way and stay away from me."

There was more laughter as I pushed past them and stalked down the path. I was almost to the gate when I saw Rich standing there.

"I can understand those jerks doing this," I said, trying not to cry, "but I thought you were my friend. Back where I come from, friends are people you can trust. My friends would never do something like this."

He went to grab my arm. "Amber, listen, I didn't—"

But I shook him off. "Just stay away from me!" I yelled. "Don't come near me again. This just shows me what I've known all along. I hate it here!"

I pushed past him and started to run down the street. I heard him yelling after me, but I just ran faster and faster until I got home.

Katie and Beau were in the front hall with my father. They'd been at a Halloween party at Katie's school.

"Amber, what happened?" my dad asked.

"You did this!" I yelled. "You brought me here and put me through this. My entire life is ruined. I'll never be happy again until you let me go back where I belong!"

Chapter Ten

A S I LAY miserably curled in a ball with my com-
forter over my head, I vowed that I wouldn't
make the same mistake again. For one stupid moment
I had started to think I could be happy in Wyoming
after all, but now I knew that just wasn't going to happen. I hated it there and I was not going to make
friends with anyone, especially not Rich Winter. As
far as I was concerned, he didn't exist anymore. I'd
never forgive him. Never, never, never.

My mother told me that Rich had called several
times, but I told her I never wanted to speak to him
again. And I meant it, too. On the school bus I sat
alone and read a book all the way to school. I didn't
look up once. Every time I saw Rich looking or heading in my direction, I turned away. I had planned to
drop cheerleading too, but when I told Mary Jo, she
was devastated.

"Amber, you can't quit on us now. You just can't," she said.

"Why should I do anything for this dumb school?" I demanded. "I can't wait to go back to New York, where people are civilized."

"Okay, so the guys played a dumb joke on you," she said. "They always do that to new kids. There was no real harm in it. They were just trying to put you in your place because you got all the glory at the game the other day." She gave me a hopeful and apologetic smile. "You know what big egos football players have."

"Some of them, maybe, but there's one I can't forgive."

"Who?"

"Rich Winter. Just when it seemed . . ." I broke down as a big sob threatened to explode from my throat. I took a deep breath. "I really thought he liked me, Mary Jo."

"Oh, Amber, I'm sure Rich—" Mary Jo began.

I shook my head firmly. "It's just like it was when I came here before. I liked Rich then and thought we were having fun together. But then he put his horrible frog down my back."

Mary Jo looked horrified. "When was this?"

"When I was ten," I confessed.

Mary Jo's lips quivered and she burst out laughing. "Oh, Amber. All ten-year-old boys do dumb stuff."

"But they're supposed to grow out of it by the time they're sixteen," I said. "Don't worry. I won't give them any more chances. I'm staying away from Rich and all his moronic football buddies. In fact, I'm staying away from everybody. I just want to be left alone."

She looked hurt. "So you're really not going to work with the cheerleaders anymore? We won't be able to go to the state championship after all?"

"How do I know you weren't all in on that stupid Halloween prank?" I demanded, knowing it wasn't true.

"Amber, I swear none of us knew about it, or we would have warned you. Girls have to stick together at our school. The boys want to run everything and have their own way. That's how it's always been. That's why it was so incredible that we were getting a chance to go to the state championship this year."

"Okay," I said gruffly. "I'll work with you guys during lunch every day, but that's all I'm doing."

So that's exactly what I did. I worked with Mary Jo and the other cheerleaders on the field on sunny days and in the gym on wet ones. And after school I rode home with my nose in a book, did my homework, and went to bed. Thrilling life, right? That was what I wrote to Brendan.

You don't have to worry about me meeting anybody out here, I wrote. *There is not one guy I'd look at twice. They are all brainless, juvenile creeps with a mental age of about two.* I could picture Brendan sitting on a bench in Central Park, looking at me in that special way. *I miss you so much,* I wrote.

I picked up his last letter and reread it. Lots of news about teachers at school, how Suzanne had bluffed her way into a dance club with a fake ID. But nothing about how he was feeling, or how much he was missing me. Sighing, I put the letter down.

Our phone calls hadn't been too successful, either. I'd begged to have an extension put in my room, but so far I'd had to make my calls from the front hall, freezing cold and with everyone listening to every word I said. Brendan had promised to call every night, but by then it was down to about one short call a week.

I sucked on my pen and stared out the window. Fall was turning into winter. The yellow leaves had turned brown and now lay in great drifts across the yard, leaving bare bones of trees behind. The mountains were no longer just tipped with snow; it lay in shining white sheets, reaching almost down to the trees. There was frost in the mornings, making the fields glisten. I suppose fall turned into winter back home too, but I'd never noticed it there. The central heating had been automatically turned on in our building, and we'd put on winter coats when it got cold and used umbrellas when it rained, but that had been all.

Other minor miracles started to happen. Mom's bread became edible. Dad took his old desk from my room up to the attic and sat up there with a kerosene stove for heat, the words *Chapter One* typed on his laptop. Katie had been promised a pet lamb in the spring by a schoolmate and Beau no longer came home showing signs of his latest fight. In fact, he was rapidly becoming the class wise guy and know-it-all, and he loved it!

So I guess you could say we were all settling in by the time the first snow came. It took us by surprise, waking us one morning to cold blue light and a landscape changed beyond recognition. The cattle stood huddled in one corner of the field, looking sorry for themselves, their breath coming like clouds of steam. The snow came over my boots as I made my way to the road, and the school bus was fifteen minutes late. Some kids didn't even make it to school that day, their farms cut off until the snowplows could get there. And lots of people were home with the flu.

I thought we were all pretty healthy—we'd rarely been sick in New York. But one night Beau said that his throat hurt and Dad said his hurt, too. The next morning they were both running fevers, and Mom had a bad headache.

I kept waiting for the sore throat or the headache to start, but nothing happened. By the end of the week Grandpa and I were the only members of the household not in bed.

"Okay, Amber, it's all up to you now," he said, appearing in the kitchen as I was trying to make herbal tea for the patients upstairs.

"What's up to me?"

"Everything. The ranch. I'm still useless with this leg, so I'm going to have to rely on you. We need more firewood before you go to school, and don't forget to bring in the milk and feed the chickens, will you?"

"What do you think I am, a slave?" I demanded. "Slavery went out with Abe Lincoln."

"Someone has to do it," he said. "All the other kids around here can handle a few simple chores. Some of them have to milk an entire dairy herd before school." He indicated the door. "Go fetch the milk and firewood and I'll finish making breakfast."

I put on my coat and boots and stomped to the end of the track to get the milk. Then I found that there were only a couple of logs already cut when I went to get some wood. I'd never chopped wood before in my life. In fact, even with my strong feminist principles, I believed that chopping wood was a man's job. But, as Grandpa had said, someone had to do it. The house just wasn't warm enough without a big fire. I gritted my teeth and went to find the ax. I found a likely log, swung with all my might, and felt the ax bounce off again without leaving so much as a dent in the wood.

"I will not be beaten by you!" I muttered, and turned the log end up. I swung and swung again. Suddenly it fell apart into two pieces. After half an hour, during which I missed taking off my toe by millimeters, I staggered back into the house with the wood.

"I suppose that will have to do," Grandpa muttered.

"Have to do?" I burst out. "I'm going to miss the school bus if I don't hurry. I have no time to fix my hair or my makeup, and you can't even say thank you? Girls aren't supposed to chop wood, you know."

"Is that a fact?" he said, and I saw him grinning as I stomped out to throw corn to the dumb chickens. When I got back inside, Grandpa pointed to a tray. "You'd better take their breakfasts up," he said. "I can't make the stairs yet."

I was beginning to feel as if I were trapped in one of those dreams where there is no escape. I swept up the tray, slopping tea all over, and made my way up

103

the stairs. My entire family were lying in their beds, groaning. Nobody wanted the eggs that Grandpa had made and nobody thanked me for bringing up their food. I knew exactly how Cinderella had felt. If a fairy godmother didn't appear in the near future, I was definitely considering running away!

As I reached the main road the school bus was already beginning to pull out. I screamed, and the bus stopped again. Laughing faces pressed against the windows, yelling out dumb remarks as I ran to catch it.

"What happened—overslept?" Rich asked sweetly.

I just gave him my most withering stare.

I could hardly stay awake in my classes all day and I was bone-tired by the time I trudged home. Grandpa had made soup, and my first chore was to take it up to the sick ones. Then I had to split more logs, take up more hot tea . . . It was like being a hamster in one of those little wheels. The faster I ran, the more chores there seemed to be. Around nine o'clock I was about to go upstairs to bed when the phone rang. It was Brendan.

"We're all at a party at Mandy's place and we thought we'd give you a call," he said brightly. "We're having a blast. Listen to the new Smashing Pumpkins CD Mandy got." He held the phone away from him and a mixture of loud music and laughter rang in my ear. "Like it? Here's Suzanne to say hi."

"Wait, Brendan. I need to talk to—" I began, but he had already passed the phone to someone else.

One by one my friends came to the phone. "Hi,

Amber. We miss you! Wish you could be here . . ."

I felt a tear begin to trickle down my cheek, and I realized when they hung up that nobody had asked me what *my* Friday night was like. I went up to bed, pulled my quilt over me, and fell into an exhausted sleep.

Next morning it was the same thing all over again—logs, chickens, milk, breakfast trays. Luckily it was Saturday. When I'd finished eating my own breakfast, Grandpa faced me across the table. "Do you know how to drive yet?" he demanded.

"No. Dad didn't want me to learn in the city, and I'm not sixteen yet."

Grandpa grunted, as if this confirmed that I was hopeless. "Well, you must have some idea," he said. "Someone's going to have to take feed up to the cattle. It should have been done a couple of days ago, but your pa's been sick. All you have to do is load up the trailer and then take the tractor up into the pasture. Nothing hard about it. I'll see if I can get across the yard to help you start it up."

"I can't drive a tractor and a trailer!" I exclaimed in horror. I had seen the monster tractor when Dad drove it. "I've never even driven a car yet."

"The cattle can't starve," Grandpa said. "And tractors are easier than cars."

We made our way slowly across the snowy yard to the barn. The tractor looked even bigger than I remembered it. It took all my strength to load the trailer with bales of hay, and my legs were trembling as I climbed up into the high seat.

"Okay, turn the key and give it some gas,"

Grandpa said, standing below. "That pedal there. Harder. Give it a good kick."

The engine sprang to life with a roar. The whole tractor was shaking up and down. "Now put your clutch in—no, not that foot! The other one! And put it into first gear . . . across and up. Put some muscle into it. There, that's right. Now let the clutch out slowly, and off you go."

I brought up the pedal, and the tractor jerked forward without stalling. It chugged painfully slowly across the yard and up the track. At the end of the track was a gate. I managed to put the brake on while I climbed down and opened it, then I took off again, bumping and lurching over the snowy ground. There were a few cattle at that end of the pasture, but most were way at the far end—little brown dots on the hillside against the white of the snow.

I kept on going for a while before I stopped again, clambered onto the trailer, and pushed the first bale of hay off. I repeated this a couple more times and then suddenly I found that I was driving into deep snow. As the snow came over the wheels the tractor sputtered and stalled. I couldn't get it going again. I really didn't want to climb down into the snow—it was a long walk back to the house, and I was sure Grandpa would yell at me for leaving his precious tractor out in the field.

I sat there, not knowing what to do next. "Okay, fairy godmother, where are you when I need you?" I wondered aloud.

At that moment there was a shout behind me and

the sound of a horse galloping across the snow. "Hey there," a man yelled. "Your gate's open and the cattle are out!"

As he drew even with me I wasn't entirely surprised to find it was Rich. "You left the gate open," he yelled accusingly. "You've got cattle wandering off."

"Oh, great!" I yelled. "That's just great. One more thing to make my day!"

He looked at me in surprise, as if he'd just recognized who I was. "Amber? What are you doing out here?"

"Good question," I said. "I was asking myself the same thing. It wasn't my idea, believe me. My crabby grandfather informed me that the cattle had to be fed and there was nobody else to do it, just the same as there was nobody else to chop wood, feed the chickens—you name it, I do it."

"What about your parents?"

"They're sick," I said. "Everyone has the flu except me and Grandpa."

"So you're stuck with all the chores?" he said with sympathy. "Hey, that's tough. I was heading into town, but hold on a moment and I'll round up your cattle for you. Then I'll come give you a hand."

I could only sit there, waiting and watching. A little later he appeared with five steers running ahead of him. He threw down a bale of hay for them and they started eating.

"Now, just start the tractor and back it up slowly," he said.

"I can't get it started and I don't know how to back up. I've never driven before," I said.

"You don't know how to drive?"

I shook my head.

"Then I'd say you've done pretty well to get this far," he said. "Come on, get down and hold my horse and I'll get the tractor out of the drift for you."

He slid off his horse and waded through the deep snow to the tractor. Then he held his arms up to me. He lifted me as if I weighed nothing at all and waded back through the snow with me in his arms.

I was conscious of his warmth and closeness and his strength supporting me. "You don't eat enough, girl," he said with a laugh. "I could carry you from here clean to Cody."

"I wish you'd carry me clean to New York," I said.

"I would if I could," he said. "If I thought it would make you happy."

"Oh, right," I said with a bitter laugh. "You'll probably carry me until you come to the deepest snowdrift and then you'll drop me and get another good laugh at my expense. If you like, I'll wait while you go call your buddies so they can laugh, too."

"Amber, what are you talking about?" he asked, lowering me gently to the ground.

"As if you don't know. I saw you there on Halloween. You were with all those dumb guys watching me nearly die of terror and then fall in the cold stream. I bet you got a real kick out of it, the way you did with that frog."

"Would you forget about that frog?" he said. "I was ten years old, for Pete's sake, and I did it because I didn't know how to tell you I liked you."

"You *liked* me? You had a funny way of showing it."

"I know," he said. "I was a dumb kid. I didn't know how to handle girls. But I wasn't in on that Halloween stunt, whatever you may think."

"Well, I saw you," I said shakily. He was still standing very close to me.

"You saw me come running up the path to warn you," he corrected. "Only, I got there too late. I was over at a friend's house when I heard what they were planning to do. I drove to your house but you'd already left, so I ran like crazy to the Samson place . . . and I was too late. You didn't give me a chance to explain."

Rich had wanted to help me. To come to my rescue. "No," I said slowly, "I didn't give you a chance to explain. I thought you were in on it." I gazed up at his strong face, his cheeks red from the cold air. "I'm sorry," I said.

"It's okay," he said. His face creased into a smile that showed adorable laugh lines at the sides of his eyes. "I guess I'd have felt the same if someone whisked me off to the middle of New York City. Especially if it was away from my *friends*," he added, emphasizing the last word.

"I think I'm learning to survive pretty well without those friends," I said hesitantly. "And New York is so very far away."

We stood there looking at each other. It was as if there were an invisible electric ray going between us.

"So you think you might be willing to give things out here in the boonies a chance after all?" he asked softly.

109

"I think I'd be dumb if I didn't," I said.

A loud *moo* sounded right behind us, startling us both back to reality. "Dumb cattle," Rich growled. "They're complaining that we haven't put out the rest of the feed yet. Come on, let's get this old tractor started up before she freezes solid, and then you can drive while I put out the hay." He hopped up to the seat.

I stood there watching and wondering. If the steer hadn't interrupted us, I think that Rich would have kissed me just then.

Chapter Eleven

RICH GOT THE tractor started, and I drove slowly up the rest of the slope with him on the trailer, throwing out bales of hay at regular intervals.

"That should keep 'em happy for a few days," he said. "Now let's see you take the tractor back by yourself." He seemed so confident that I could do it.

I was able to drive all the way back into the yard while he followed behind on his horse.

"Okay," he said, tying the horse to the gatepost. "What other chores need doing?"

"Don't you have to be somewhere else?" I asked.

"Are you trying to get rid of me?"

"Are you crazy? I'd keep Frankenstein's monster if he was willing to help me."

Rich laughed. "Very good, mistress. I am yours to command!" He started doing a monster walk toward the house.

I ran to keep up with him. "Rich, it's really nice of you and I do appreciate it, but weren't you on your way to something when you first saw me?"

"It can wait," he said, smiling.

My stomach did a tiny flip-flop. "In that case," I said, "I'd love some help with the wood. I'm terrible at splitting logs."

"These don't look too bad," he said, noting the pathetic few that I'd done earlier. "You've gotten the hang of this real quick." He took a log and split it with one easy swing.

"Oh, right," I said, laughing at my own feeble attempts. "I've sure gotten the hang of it. It takes me half an hour to get a few miserable pieces."

"Ah, but I've had to do this all my life," Rich said. "You've had to learn a lot in a hurry."

"You can say that again," I agreed. As I gathered up an armful of firewood I went over what I had done—the tractor and the hay bales and the wood, as well as looking after four sick people. I was pretty impressed with myself. It was the first time in my life I'd had to do something really hard, and I'd managed it. In New York, I'd always expected someone to take care of me while I had fun. I'd never had to do anything that really challenged me like that. It felt real. And I was proud.

"Let's take this load inside, and then we'll see what else needs to be done," Rich said.

"This is really nice of you, Rich," I said again.

"We always help our neighbors around here," he said. "It's part of the code of the hills."

At first I thought he was serious. But then I saw his eyes twinkling. "Shut up," I said, laughing as I nudged him along. "I don't believe you're the back-woods type of person you make yourself out to be."

Rich grinned and went ahead of me into the house.

"Now that's more like it," I heard Grandpa say to him. "Did she get my tractor back in one piece, Rich?"

"She sure did, Mr. Stevens," Rich said. "Handled it like a pro. You've got one handy granddaughter here."

"I was thinking the same thing," Grandpa said. "Reminds me a lot of her grandma."

I stood in the hallway and looked at my grandfather with surprise. So he really didn't think I was a useless klutz after all. But why couldn't he come out and say any of those nice things to me in person? He'd built a wall up around himself and he wasn't about to take it down in a hurry. When I came into the room with the second armful of wood, Grandpa looked at me with an expressionless face. "Lose any toes today?" he growled. "Or has Rich shown you the right way to do it?"

"I'm showing her the right way to do a lot of things," Rich said, his eyes flirting with me so shamelessly that I blushed, even though I didn't have any reason to. "What else needs to be done, Mr. Stevens?"

"If you're offering, I was thinking that someone ought to clear that driveway, just in case there's any more snow on the way."

"No problem," Rich said. "Come on, Amber. Show me where the shovels are. This will build up your muscles."

113

A month earlier I would have complained like crazy about having to shovel a driveway. But somehow it seemed like fun that day. I headed for the front door, switching my damp gloves for some nice dry ones. "Last one there is a rotten egg," I yelled, and we both scrambled across the front hallway, reaching the front door at the same time and fighting to get through, giggling and shrieking.

"Don't make so much noise," came Beau's protesting voice from upstairs. "I've got a headache! And while you're there, would you bring me up a bowl of chili and some chips and some ice cream?"

"Sounds like someone is getting better," Rich commented, grinning as he stood back to let me through the door first.

"If you're better enough for chili, you're better enough to come down here yourself," I called. No answer.

We found shovels and worked on the deep snow at the bottom of the drive. It was very hard work. After a while the snow seemed as heavy as cement, and my back felt as if it were about to break. But Rich was there right beside me, working ten times as hard as I was.

"Hey, Amber," he said when I was just about to call it quits. I looked up, and a snowball caught me right in the face.

"You're asking for it now," I yelled, and scooped up a generous snowball of my own. I threw it at him.

"Missed me!" he yelled.

"Stupid game," I muttered. "We won't get this driveway finished before dark if we don't get back to work."

I started shoveling again—and watched him out of the corner of my eye as I worked. I quietly scooped up snow in my hands, and just when he was bending down to lift a huge load, I crept up behind him and shoved it down his collar.

"That's for putting a frog down my back!" I shrieked, dancing around delightedly as he hollered.

"You're going to get it now, girl," he said. I threw down my shovel as he came after me. I tried to run, but the snow was awfully deep, and Rich could run faster. We came back toward the house. The yard with the barn and shed was on my right, and there was a fence between me and it. I'd known all those years of gymnastics were going to be useful someday. I approached the fence and vaulted it.

"No fair!" he yelled. "I forgot that dumb circus stuff."

We stood there with the fence between us, laughing defiantly at each other.

"Come on back," he said. "We need to get this shoveling finished."

"Only if you promise not to throw any more snowballs."

"Okay. I promise," he said. I climbed onto the fence, and Rich held out his hands to catch me as I jumped down. We stood there, holding hands.

"You've got snowflakes on your eyelashes," he said at last. "They make you look awful pretty."

"Am I going to get that driveway finished today or not?" Grandpa roared from the doorway. "And you'd better ask that young man if he wants to have lunch.

You haven't eaten, and it's almost three o'clock. I've made a big pot of stew."

I looked inquiringly at Rich. "Weren't you supposed to be doing things today?"

"Nah. Nothing that can't wait," he said.

We finished our task and then walked in companionable silence up the driveway as the sun painted yellow stripes across the snow. Grandpa had the table set and we fell on huge bowls of food, practically finishing them before pausing to talk.

Rich looked across at me. "I was wondering," he said slowly. "If you're not doing anything special this evening, would you like to . . . I thought maybe you'd like to do something together. Just hang out, get out of the house?"

"Sure," I said. "That would be great. I'll go get changed out of these disgusting clothes. I'll be just a few minutes."

Before I did, I took up a final tray to the invalids. I could tell they were getting better because they all complained that they didn't like stew. Beau wanted pizza and Katie wanted chocolate ice cream. I took a quick shower and changed into jeans without rips in the knees and a pretty silk shirt, my hair still damp from a quick blow-dry.

"Hey, that was pretty fast. I was going to suggest dancing," he said, nodding with approval as I came back into the room, "but then I thought you've probably had enough physical activity for one day."

I nodded. "You're right. I don't think I could

make my legs dance right now. I don't even know if they'll make it as far as your truck."

"How about a movie, then?"

"A movie? Is there a movie theater in town?"

"Not exactly," he said, looking embarrassed. "But we could rent something for the VCR."

"That sounds just as good to someone who has been TV-starved for weeks now," I said. "You'll be okay, Grandpa?" I asked.

"Go ahead. Enjoy yourselves, you've earned it," he said.

"Come on, let's go," Rich said as he took my hand.

Rich rode his horse home and returned with his truck.

We drove twenty-five miles into town to the video store and picked out a movie we both liked. I would have thought Rich would be all for action and violence, but he liked old romantic comedies. So we settled on *A Room with a View*.

"I've always wanted to see this one," he said, "but my family would have teased the heck out of me if I'd brought it home."

"I see," I said, smiling at his discomfort. "So now you've got me to blame it on."

"You've got it," he admitted, grinning too.

"I wouldn't have thought this was your kind of movie," I said as we walked back to the truck. "Too slow and sentimental."

"I've always dreamed of going to Italy one day," Rich admitted as he helped me climb into the truck. "I was thinking of getting a tape to teach myself Italian."

117

"Really?"

"Yeah. Dumb dream, I suppose."

"Not at all. It's great to have dreams," I said. "Why Italy?"

He shrugged sheepishly. "Someone I used to know went there once. She told me about it."

"Was this Emily?"

"Yeah," he said in surprise. "How did you know about her?"

"The girls at cheerleading told me."

He sighed. "I guess it's common knowledge around school. I took it pretty hard when she moved away. Nothing seemed the same."

"You haven't been to visit her since she left?"

He shook his head. "No money. I started to save up, but then I stopped. It wouldn't be the same. Her dad's a painter—they always had artsy people visiting, and they only listened to classical music. I guess it got too boring for them out here. They moved to New England—somewhere in Connecticut. Not too far from New York City, right?"

"Right," I agreed. The revelation about Emily had caught me by surprise. I had been imagining her as the farm girl next door who moved away to another farm, and all this time her father was a painter. Suddenly I felt threatened by this unknown Emily, even though I could have sworn I didn't want Rich for myself. I wanted to think of him as the simple farm boy, dazzled by my New York ways. But he'd already dated someone more hip than I was, someone who had been to Italy. "That's weird, isn't it?" I said, trying

118

to sound light and carefree. "The girl you love moves close to the boy I love."

"You really love him, then, this guy back in New York?"

That threw me. "I'm not quite sure what love really means yet," I said. "We didn't get to be together long enough to find out if it was more than a crush. All I know is he was very special to me. He made me feel special."

"I really loved Emily," Rich said simply. "I felt like my heart would break when she went away. For a long while I thought I'd never risk getting close to anyone ever again, because it hurt so much."

"But now?"

"Now I'm beginning to think that you can't live in the past forever," he said. "I've got a whole life ahead of me. Lots of dreams and plans to fulfill—finish high school, go to a Big Ten college. And I should be getting on with those plans, not thinking about what I can't have anymore."

"Maybe you're right," I said slowly. I was thinking about when Brendan had called from the party. He'd obviously been having a good time there without me. Maybe he'd even kissed another girl. Was I dumb to remain true to him? Was I dumb even to want to go back to New York?

We got back to Rich's house to find the place in darkness.

"Looks like my folks went out for the evening," he commented. "That's good."

Alarm bells went off in my head. Rich seemed like a

nice enough guy, but had he planned it all along? Did he know we'd be all alone in a deserted house? Was that the way those supposedly simple farm boys operated? Maybe he thought New York girls were fast and loose.

He gave me his hand to help me from the truck. "Now we won't have to fight over the VCR," he said.

"Make yourself at home," Rich said once we'd walked into his house. "I'm pretty sweaty—a shower is definitely in order." He led me into the living room, and ran upstairs.

Rich's house was really nice—cozy and comfortable. There were lots of family photographs around. And lots of trophies—Rich had won everything there was to win. Just looking at them all made me dizzy.

"Wow, you took less time than I did," I said as Rich bounded back into the room less than fifteen minutes later. He was wearing jeans and a gray sweatshirt, and his freshly shampooed hair smelled like tart apples.

"Wouldn't want you to get bored," he said, motioning me to follow him.

We made popcorn in his big, warm kitchen and then we settled down on an old overstuffed sofa. Two friendly German shepherds that had been outside came to sit at our feet and pounced on the popcorn that fell as we ate.

The movie was as good as I remembered from the first time, gentle and romantic and funny, with beautiful music and lovely Italian views. Rich sat close to me, but not touching. Then, in the middle of the story, when the heroine returns home to England and announces her engagement to someone else, Rich

120

turned to me angrily. "That's so stupid, to let some-one get away because you can't tell them what you really feel. To let other people tell you what to do! To risk ruining your whole life . . ."

We were sitting there, our knees touching, looking at each other. "Amber," he said softly, "New York is very far from here. So is Connecticut."

"Yes, it is," I said hesitantly.

"Who knows if you'll ever get back there again—or if I'll ever make it out east? And if we do, would it ever work again? Would we want it to?"

A gorgeous voice was singing Puccini on the movie soundtrack.

"I don't think I'd want it to," Rich whispered. "And I don't think you do, either."

"Maybe I don't," I whispered back.

"This is what I want to work," Rich murmured, moving closer to me. Slowly, as if drawn by invisible strings, his lips met mine. Brendan's kisses had made me tingle all over and given me a thrilling, not-quite-in-control feeling . . . as if my body had been respond-ing with a will of its own. Rich's kiss made me feel quite different. It was like a warm glow that started at my lips and spread throughout my whole body, en-closing me in a beautiful pink bubble. I never wanted it to end.

When I finally opened my eyes, I saw Rich gazing down at me, his eyes warm and glowing.

"If you try to hotfoot it back to New York, Miss Amber Stevens," he said, "I'm going to throw you over my saddle and ride off into the mountains with you."

121

"You mountain men are very aggressive," I said, my eyes teasing him.

"You'd better believe it," he said. "We don't ever give up without a fight. My family was involved in the range wars, way back when—cattle versus sheep. Those outsiders tried to drive us off our land and cut off our water rights, but we stayed put and we're still here, long after those intruders left."

I was about to make some flippant comment about that, but suddenly it hit me: I came from that heritage too. My ancestors had probably fought in those range wars alongside Rich's. I shared that same stubborn determination, that willingness to fight for what I believed in.

"Rich," I reminded him, "we're missing the movie. It's just getting to the good part."

He laughed. "To heck with the movie," he said. "We're just getting to the good part too." Then he pulled me to him and this time the kiss was neither gentle or hesitant. It left me breathless, my heart pounding.

After what seemed like only a few minutes, I looked up to find that the movie had ended, and that the clock on the mantelpiece said almost eleven.

"I guess I'd better drive you home," Rich said, pulling me to my feet.

"I hope I don't get in trouble," I began, but Rich laughed. "Your grandpa will be the only one awake, and he thinks I'm a good guy. He'll be glad that we're teaming up."

"You make us sound like mules," I said.

He ruffled my hair and laughed. We sat very close together in the truck driving home. It was so cold my breath hung in the air like smoke.

"I'll be over in the morning to see if any chores need to be done," Rich said. "And then do you want to go for a ride? I need to exercise Blackbird. I didn't get much chance all week."

"I don't know how to ride a horse," I confessed, torn between my desire to be with him all day and the reality that I'd probably fall off and look like a fool.

"That's okay. You gotta learn sometime," he said. "You can ride old Traveler. We've got this big old Western saddle—you couldn't fall out of that if you tried."

"Well, okay," I said. "Just as long as we don't go where anyone from school can see us. I don't want to be laughed at."

"Don't worry," Rich said. "I know the perfect way to go."

He gave me a little kiss on the forehead as I climbed down from the truck. "See you tomorrow," I called.

My grandfather was waiting with the door half open. "What are you doing coming home all hours of the night?" he asked. "I suppose midnight is early for city folk."

"We had to watch the end of a movie," I lied. "You didn't have to wait up."

"Hmph," he said. "Go on, off to bed with you or you'll be useless in the morning."

I darted over and gave Grandpa a peck on his cheek. "Good night, Grandpa," I said.

"Get away with you," he said, wiping his cheek off. I could tell he was glad I'd been with Rich.

Chapter Twelve

T HE NEXT MORNING Rich arrived around nine-thirty, and we finished the chores in record time. It was a warm day and the snow was melting fast.

"All that hard work on the driveway for nothing," I said, pointing to the driveway.

"I wouldn't say that," Rich answered, gazing into my eyes. "Without all that snow, I doubt you would have given me the time of day yesterday—or last night," he teased.

After saying good-bye to everyone, we drove over to Rich's house and I met his parents.

"I'm so happy to finally meet you," Rich's mom said. She was tall and pretty, and her hair was the same color as Rich's. "He's done nothing but talk about you since you got here. I was real impressed with the way he said you were handling that big spread all alone, with everyone sick. I'm glad you're taking a day off. Here," she said, giving Rich a saddlebag. "I packed you a little snack in case you get hungry on the ride." The bag was packed with what looked like supplies for a week-long trek.

"I thought we'd have a picnic lunch up at Cascade Meadow," Rich said.

"Oh, Rich, that will be all snowed in, won't it?" his mother asked, looking worried.

"Nah, it's always sheltered there."

"Just be careful of avalanches, then," his mother warned.

"Mom. We're only going down the road, for Pete's sake," he said, rolling his eyes at me in despair. "It will be fine," he tried to reassure me.

I was feeling very nervous about getting on a horse. My only horse experience had been at a farm in New England. I'd tried to feed my apple to a horse in a field and it had snapped at me. I was even more nervous when I saw Traveler.

"He's huge!" I exclaimed. "And he looks so fierce." Traveler looked like one of those old war horses: great big head, bulging muscles. I just pictured him galloping off down the valley with me clinging helplessly to the saddle horn.

"Him? He's a big old softie," Rich said. He gave me a reassuring smile as he helped me up into the saddle. "Don't worry," he said. "You'll be just fine."

We set off, away from the houses and up the valley. The snow was melting all along the road and there was the sound of running water in the ditches. The horses' hooves made a satisfying crunch as they sank into the snow. The sun on our backs was really warm. Traveler plodded forward with big, even steps, and the saddle came up around me, holding me in place. As Rich had said, it would be practically impossible to fall off.

After a couple of miles we left the road and headed up a narrow path among the trees. A small stream cascaded down, leaping from rock to rock with a light splashing sound. Everything smelled so clean and fresh. The sky through the pine branches was a deep, clear blue, dotted with white puffball clouds, and the snow on the branches was a dazzling white.

The path continued to climb, higher and higher. There were big rocks beside us now and a rock wall up ahead. Traveler was surefooted and just kept on plodding behind Blackbird. We passed through a narrow slit between huge rocks and came out into the most perfect mountain meadow. Patches of green grass showed through the blanket of snow. At one end a waterfall danced down the rock to form the little stream that crossed the meadow. It was ringed with tall, stately trees, except for one side, where the view went on forever with range after range of hills melting into the blue distance. One ribbon of smoke curling into the clear sky was the only sign that we were not the only beings on the planet.

"How do you like it?" Rich asked in a whisper.

"It's perfect," I said quietly. It seemed the sort of place to whisper.

"I had it landscaped especially for you," Rich said. He slid from his horse and reached up his arms to me.

At the sound of our voices two deer looked up from their feeding and trotted off into the forest.

"Our own private world," I whispered, slipping off the horse.

Rich's arms were still around me, and he was looking down at me so tenderly that I thought I might melt. Gently he drew me closer and gave me a long, warm kiss. "Know what I want now?" he whispered.

"No."

"Food," he said, and made a grab for the saddlebag. He brushed the last remnants of snow from a large, flat rock and spread a rug over it. The midday sun was warm on my face.

"We could stay up here for a week," I commented as I took out some cold chicken salad, half an apple pie, a thermos of hot tomato soup, brownies, and two bananas.

"Fine with me," Rich said, giving me a wicked grin. "Just you and me in our own little shelter. If it snows again, I could build us an ice cave."

"Thanks, but no thanks," I said, throwing a crumb in his direction.

"Ice caves are really warm. I camped in one once."

"Give me central heating any day. I'm a New Yorker at heart, remember."

He looked at me long and hard. "No, I'd say you were one of us at heart," he said. "The New York outside layer is already beginning to wear off."

We ate steadily, without talking. I hadn't realized how hungry I was. Then we lay back on the blanket, my head on Rich's shoulder, and watched the clouds sailing over the white mountain peaks and the birds in the pine trees. I was feeling comfortable and drowsy until the sun dipped behind a big rock and suddenly it got very cold.

Slowly we made our way down as the pink twilight deepened into dark red. There were already lights on in the houses ahead as we rode back to civilization.

"Have a good time?" Rich's mother greeted us as we stomped into the kitchen.

"It was the most perfect day of my life," I said.

When I got to school on Monday morning, everyone knew about me and Rich. Talk about the grapevine in action!

"We're all so happy for you, Amber," Mary Jo said.

I was happy for me, too. Rich was wonderful—more wonderful than I'd ever imagined. And not only that, but I was suddenly the envy of all the girls in the school.

"What are you going to tell that guy back in New York?" Mary Beth asked.

"I . . . haven't decided yet," I said. "I need to think about that."

"New York is so far away," Mary Jo said, giving me a knowing dig. "Who knows if you'll ever see him again?"

She was right. I decided I wouldn't say anything to Brendan. The truth was, I didn't know what I felt about him anymore.

I didn't exactly mention to my family that Rich and I were now more than friends. But they weren't stupid. By the time he'd called three days in a row and then hung out with me every evening, they began to get the picture.

My family accepted the news about Rich with great relief. At least I wouldn't be bugging them about going back to New York the very next day!

Things were moving along well at home. Dad had completed four chapters of his novel. And Mom had started to do some free-lance work. Grandpa had his cast removed and started stomping around, getting his legs back in working order. Within a couple of days he was tossing hay bales about and demonstrating the correct way to chop wood. My days had never been fuller—not only did I have homework and cheerleading and chores, I had Rich.

One cold winter day I stayed late at school to watch our football team beat the Sheridan Mustangs in the semifinal game. When I got home, my dad was coming down from the attic.

"We won, Dad!" I said. "Rich scored the winning touchdown."

"Congratulations," my father said. "You've really blossomed since we moved here. I bet you'll miss all this when you go back to Dover."

"What? We're moving back to New York?" I stammered.

"Not us. You. You told us you were only giving it a year. You still want to go back, don't you?"

I didn't know what to say. I thought about the fun I was having at school. But then I thought of the art classes and drama and French and advanced science I wasn't getting. What chance would I have of getting into a good college from Indian Valley High? And Brendan and Suzanne and Mandy . . . friends who spoke my language, who knew that mocha was a kind of coffee and not a card game, and that jeans with holes in them were very cool.

"I don't know. I guess so," I said slowly. "I still have time to decide. Don't I?"

"Sure," Dad said. "It's up to you."

I gave him a kiss and hurried up to my room. Dover seemed so far away. I couldn't imagine my life without Rich. And I didn't want to.

Chapter Thirteen

As Christmas approached we were all very busy. We'd had a family conference and Mom had suggested that we forget about commercialism and make our own Christmas gifts that year. "These will be gifts from the heart," she said.

I was having a tough time coming up with things I could make well enough to be gifts. I'd gotten an old bottle and made an interesting design with different colors of candle wax over the sides for Mom. For Dad's writing projects, I'd covered a box with magazine pictures and labeled it Ideas. A publisher was interested in Dad's work, and so he was even more determined to make it a money-earning venture. That way we could stay with Grandpa on the farm and still have money coming in.

I'd tried knitting Grandpa a scarf, but it was barely six inches long. And with only five days until

Christmas, I got the feeling it wasn't going to get much longer, at my knitting pace. I'd made Katie a cardboard crown with some old fake jewels stuck on it and Beau a papier-mâché money box shaped like a pig.

When I examined my gifts in the cold light of day, I had to admit they didn't look too wonderful, even if they were gifts from the heart. I was tempted to get a ride into Cody with Rich and at least buy small backup gifts from the variety store there. I had to get something for Grandpa. He couldn't have a six-inch scarf, and I couldn't come up with any brilliant ideas on what I could turn it into. "Merry Christmas, Grandpa, here's a fuzzy wallet for you." Nope, the scarf had to go.

"I wish I knew what to give my grandpa," I said to Rich as we rode home from school together. "That scarf idea just isn't working out. I was thinking about getting him a dog. He told me his old dog died last year."

"Yep," Rich said. "Old Mack. He thought the world of that dog." Then he snapped his fingers. "Hey, you know what? The Johnsons have a new litter of puppies. I think they're border collies, just like your grandpa's old dog. You want to go take a look?"

So on Saturday we drove into town to visit the Johnsons. The puppies were all so cute that I had a hard time making a choice. "You have to pick one that won't be afraid of running among the cattle and getting itself kicked," said the ever-practical Rich. I ignored him and went for a black and white ball of fluff that licked me and then curled up in my lap. Rich promised to keep it over at his place until Christmas Day.

"Now that we're in town, what else do you want

to do?" Rich asked. The Johnsons were holding the puppy until we were ready to head home.

"You know what? I've decided something," I said. "If we're going to have homemade gifts, then at least we're going to eat real Christmas food." So I headed for the grocery store, and Rich disappeared on an errand of his own.

He was humming to himself as we rode home. *How can he hum?* I thought, going through agonies because I didn't know what to get him. Had he gotten me anything? I wanted to give him something special, but I didn't want to embarrass him. I wished I had started knitting earlier—and that I was good enough at it to have made him a scarf or sweater. *That* would have been a gift from the heart.

It was when I went back into town for last-minute shopping with my dad that I found the perfect gift. It was the soundtrack to *A Room with a View*. Dad and I staggered back through the slush, laden with enough food to survive a long blizzard. Then Dad started acting weird, claiming to have forgotten something. He rushed back into the store while I froze in the car.

On Christmas Eve we went out to cut our own tree. That wasn't hard—there were about three zillion trees in our valley, and we'd all built up muscles by this point. We dragged it home on a sled across the snowy landscape, feeling like a painting from an old Christmas card. Then Mom had us string popcorn and dried cranberries to decorate it while she went back to her baking. Good smells came from the kitchen.

"I'm sure glad she's gotten better at it," Beau

133

whispered. "Can you imagine Christmas with a tableful of food we couldn't eat?"

By the time darkness fell we had the lights on the tree, making the popcorn-cranberry strings and straw stars glow. Grandpa sent me up to the attic to find his old box of ornaments. There were glass birds and trumpets that were so old the paint had worn off, exposing clear glass beneath. And there was a beautiful glass star for the top. With the big roaring fire and the tree sparkling in the window, the house looked magical. Mom had made spiced cider and gingerbread cookies, and we sat around singing songs and sharing memories.

In the morning I woke early, as I always did on Christmas Day, and started to run downstairs—until I remembered there wouldn't be a CD player or a new leather jacket under the tree that year. I couldn't imagine what sort of gifts I'd get.

Beau and Katie danced down the stairs, excited as ever.

"Come on, Mom, get up. Don't you want to open your presents?" Beau yelled.

"What's all this noise at such an ungodly hour?" Grandpa demanded. "All that fuss over a few presents?"

"Don't you like getting presents, Grandpa?" Katie asked sweetly.

"It's been so long, I've forgotten," he muttered, but he pulled her onto his knee as they sat beside the lit tree.

Dad, as usual, played Santa, and started handing out gifts. One by one we opened them.

"It's a paperweight, Dad," Beau said as Dad

opened a box to find a rock painted in bright colors.

Beau gave me sheets of paper stapled together with a flowery cover. "It's a diary, Amber, so you can write down your deep thoughts."

Mom had made me a choker from old beads she'd found in a secondhand store. Dad had made me a bookshelf. Katie got a big stuffed lamb pillow, and Beau and Katie both got small bookshelves. Grandpa didn't give us anything. Soon all the presents were unwrapped and we sat there, pretending to be excited. It was Katie who broke first.

"Is this everything?" she said in a quivering voice.

"That's right. Now how about breakfast?" Mom said brightly.

"All I'm going to get for Christmas?"

"Remember how we talked about homemade gifts being best?"

She burst into tears. "But they're not best. They're horrible," she sobbed. "This is the worst Christmas I ever had!"

Dad got up and left the room in a hurry. So did Mom. So did I. I knew just how Katie felt. It was nice to get homemade things, but they looked homemade. It wasn't the same as opening a nice Bloomingdale's box and taking out a fluffy new sweater. I sprinted up to my room, grabbed my bag of goodies, and ran down again.

"Here," I said, handing Katie and Beau each a stocking full of chocolate animals and little toys. "I got these just in case."

"Oh, wow!" Beau exclaimed.

135

"Look what Amber got us!" Katie yelled as Mom and Dad came back into the room.

"Here," Dad said, and handed out packages. "I got these just in case the handmade stuff didn't work."

"So did I," Mom said, and passed us packages of her own. As we opened toys and sweaters and music store gift certificates and the imported food items I'd bought, we started laughing at our own stupidity.

Suddenly I noticed that Grandpa was very quiet. I went over to him. "I know I didn't give you a present yet, Grandpa," I said. "It's coming later this morning."

"Didn't manage to finish knitting it in time?" he asked, a twinkle in his eye.

"What makes you think it was knitted?" I asked.

"Not much I miss in this house," he said. "And I'd like to see you in your room after breakfast, too."

"Okay," I said. Maybe he had presents for us after all and was just too shy to give them to us with everyone watching.

Breakfast was apple pancakes, fresh fruit, and hot braided spiced bread. Grandpa took one bite of the bread and looked up, surprised. "Is this what smelled so good baking last night? This is Grandma's recipe," he said, looking at Beau, Katie, and me. "She always made this at Christmas."

"I know," Mom said serenely. "I found her recipe book and I practiced until it came out perfectly."

"Tastes just like when she made it," Grandpa said, his voice shaky.

After we'd cleared the table I went to my room

and heard Grandpa's heavy step coming up the stairs pretty soon after.

"I wanted you to have this," he said gruffly, and handed me a faded velvet box. Inside was a ring of garnets and pearls set in the shape of a flower.

"It used to be your grandmother's," he said. "It was the first ring I ever bought her. I wanted to ask her to marry me, but I didn't have much money in those days, so I told her I couldn't afford diamonds. She just said, 'As if the cattle will care if I'm wearing diamonds or not.' A sensible woman, your grandmother. You remind me of her a lot—you have that look about you when you turn your head."

My eyes were brimming with tears. "Grandpa, I couldn't take this. It's too precious," I said.

"But I want you to have it," he said. "Your grandma never got to know you, but I'm sure she'd want you to wear it. You've got her grit. She always hung in there, and so do you." He looked up suddenly. "I know it hasn't been easy for you, moving here. But you've done a lot of hard stuff, and I'd say you've turned out pretty special. Just like your grandma."

I flung my arms around him. "Oh, Grandpa, it's so good to hear you say that."

Slowly his arms closed around me. "It's good to have you here," he said huskily. "It's good to be a family again. I . . . I don't ever want you to leave."

A loud honking outside made me break away and run to the window. "Grandpa, your present's just arrived!"

"You're giving me Rich Winter as a Christmas present?"

137

"No, silly, he's bringing it. Come and see," I said, dragging him downstairs.

Everyone came out onto the porch as Rich carried the box from his truck.

"Go ahead, open it," I said, handing it to Grandpa.

"Feels heavy. Have you been baking bread?" He chuckled. Then he opened the box and a little black and white nose poked out.

"A puppy!" squealed Katie.

Grandpa looked at the little dog and then at me. "Just like old Mack," he said in a broken voice. "Another little Mack. How did you know?"

I didn't want to tell him that I'd just picked the cutest puppy. So I smiled secretively.

"You couldn't have given me a better gift," he said.

As Grandpa carried the puppy into the house Dad pulled me aside. "That was pretty special, Amber. I'm proud of you." He kissed my forehead and joined everyone inside, leaving me alone with Rich.

"Seems like you made a hit there," Rich said.

"Thanks for keeping him for me. Do you want to come in for a bite to eat?" I asked.

"I can't. We're going to head to my uncle's for Christmas dinner. I wanted to see you first, though."

"Don't go yet," I said, putting my hand on his arm. "I have something for you."

"You do?"

I ran into the house and brought him the CD.

"This is so nice," he said, staring down at it. "I didn't even realize you could buy the soundtrack! And the card too." It was a scene of Venice.

"And I have something for you," he said, handing me a little package. Inside was a box and inside that was a silver locket shaped like a heart. "I hope you don't already have one," he said awkwardly.

I shook my head. "It's perfect, Rich. Please put it on for me."

I turned around as he fastened the clasp at my neck. "I'm never going to take it off," I whispered. "Thank you very much."

"Do I get a Christmas kiss?" he asked.

"I guess you deserve one," I said. I raised my face and touched my lips to his for a second.

"Is that it?"

"My brother and sister might be watching," I said. "And my parents. We don't want them to panic again and send me to Alaska this time."

"I'd come, too," he said.

"In that case," I whispered, "let them panic." And that time I really kissed him.

"Thank you again for the locket," I said as we drew apart. "It's the best present anyone has ever given me."

"I could find you a picture, if you want to put one inside," he said.

"Of what, one of your cows?" I teased.

He reached down and threw a snowball at me. I laughed and threw a much bigger one back. He grabbed my wrists. "Hey, that's enough," he said. "I'm all dressed up to go visit my relatives and I don't have time to change my clothes, so behave yourself."

"Yes, sir," I said, grinning at him.

"And you just wait until I'm not dressed up," he

said. "You want a snowball fight—you can have one!"

"Fine with me! Anytime," I called as he sprang back into the truck. I ran over to the door. "Merry Christmas, Rich. And I *would* like a picture of you to put in the locket."

"You can come over and pick one out," he said. "Oh, and I meant to tell you. A group of us always goes up to Mary Jo's cabin in the mountains for New Year's. Her parents will be there, but they're cool. It's a tradition. I really want you to come." He leaned out and kissed me again. "Merry Christmas, Amber. I . . . I think I'm falling in love with you," he said shyly, and quickly drove away.

"Merry Christmas, Rich!" I yelled, hoping the roar of his engine didn't muffle my words. "I love you too," I whispered to the back of his truck. I had never said that to anyone before . . . and I was almost glad Rich hadn't heard me. That was a huge step, and I wasn't sure either of us was ready to take it.

We were in the middle of Christmas dinner when the phone rang. "If that's your great-aunt Dorothy, tell her to call us back later," Grandpa yelled as I went to answer it. But it wasn't her.

"Amber. Merry Christmas," said a familiar male voice.

"Brendan?" I wasn't expecting his call. "Merry Christmas!"

"It's good to hear your voice," he said. "Guess what, Amber? I've got great news."

"What?"

"We were talking about you at Fiorelli's and Suzanne said, 'I know, why don't we go see her?' And we all thought it was a great idea. So we're coming."

"You're coming? Out here?"

"Yeah, isn't it fantastic? Suzanne and Thomas and Mandy and me. We're all flying out for New Year's. That's okay, isn't it? Don't tell me you're going skiing or something."

"N-no," I stammered. "No skiing."

"Great. And we'll bring sleeping bags, so you don't have to worry about beds. My dad's looking into flights. You really are in the middle of nowhere, aren't you? . . . Amber? Say something. Can you believe we're going to see each other again?"

"No, Brendan," I managed to say. "I can't. I'm overwhelmed."

I stood in the hallway cradling the phone after we'd hung up. That was one present I'd never expected. And I wasn't sure I wanted it.

Chapter Fourteen

To say that the news threw me for a loop was a total understatement. I didn't know what to do. Did I really love Rich? Then how could I still love Brendan? I couldn't be in love with two boys at the same time, could I? Rich made me feel so warm and happy and comfortable. So why was I excited at the thought of seeing Brendan again?

I remembered the way Brendan had made me feel when I looked at him. I remembered his sweet good-bye the last day we'd spent together. And I remembered how I had loved life in New York. Maybe if I had a chance to compare Brendan and Rich, I'd know who I really wanted to be with.

The unexpected news threw my entire family into a whirlwind of activity. We'd been shut away in our own little snowy world for so long that visitors from the outside seemed really exciting. Dad moved his

142

desk down to the front bedroom and Mom made up beds in the big attic room.

"The two boys can sleep in here," she said. "The two girls can put their sleeping bags in your room. You'll be up all night talking and giggling, I'm sure."

I gave her a weak smile.

"Oh, and I must start baking," she went on. "I wonder if they'd like that Christmas bread I made. And that apple Betty was good. . . ." She looked up at me. "Are you excited, honey?" she asked.

I nodded.

"You don't look very excited," she said. "All this time you've been pining for your old friends, and now that they're coming, you seem like you don't want them here."

"I do want to see them," I began, then I gave a big sigh. "Mom, what am I going to do about Brendan? What am I going to tell Rich?"

She digested this. "Yes, you do have a problem, don't you?" she said. "So you still really like Brendan? I thought you'd gotten over him. Why don't you tell him you've found someone else? I'm sure he'll understand."

Which shows you how totally clueless parents can be. "Get real, Mom. Would you want to come out all the way from New York to have someone say, 'Sorry, thanks for coming, but I've found someone else?'"

"If you'd be uncomfortable seeing him again, then the only fair thing would be to call him and tell him not to come."

"But I want to see him again," I said. "I want to see all my friends again. And I'm not sure how I feel

143

about Brendan. I mean, Rich is here now and I . . . I really like him. But maybe Brendan is really the one and I just like being with Rich because he's here. I don't know. I won't know until I spend some time with Brendan again."

"That's one I can't answer for you," Mom said. "But it seems to me you can't pull this comparison test off without hurting someone's feelings, Amber."

"I don't want to hurt either of them," I said. "I guess I want too much. I want Rich while I'm here, but if I go back to New York, then I want Brendan to be there waiting for me."

Mom laughed and ruffled my hair. "I must have brought you up to be greedy. *I* never had two boys at the same time," she said.

"I wish I didn't," I said. "Talk about complicating my life. If only I could come up with a plan."

As I finished putting clean linen on the beds it suddenly occurred to me that maybe I *could* pull it off. After all, it was only for a few days, wasn't it? Brendan and Rich never had to meet. Rich would be up at the cabin for most of the time they would be visiting. If I told Rich that some friends were arriving from New York and I'd be tied up entertaining them, he wouldn't have to know that my old boyfriend was among the group. And I'd keep quiet about Rich around Brendan. If I found that I really had gotten over Brendan, then the four days would soon be over and at least I'd know which boy to choose. It might just work!

I didn't see Rich until the next morning, when I was out on the tractor with my dad, taking feed up to the cattle in the top pasture where the snow was still deep. I looked up as I heard the call echoing across the valley.

"Hey, Amber! Yoo-hoo!" The words echoed back from the mountain walls, my name dancing at me from all sides. Rich waved his hat and then urged his horse into a gallop, flying over the snow-covered fields toward me. I thought how right he looked, riding so easily that it looked like he and the horse were one. I watched him until he reined in beside me. His cheeks were glowing from the cold wind and his hair was every which way. I'd never seen him look more handsome.

"Looks like you've gotten the hang of the tractor pretty quickly," he said appreciatively. "We'll make a rancher out of you yet. And when the snow melts, I'll teach you to drive my truck. It's real easy."

I swallowed hard as he talked about our future together. *How can I do this to him? How can I even let Brendan come here, into our world?* But then I thought of Brendan's dark eyes and the way he'd made me feel. I had to see him again so I could decide whether I still had any feelings left for him.

"Guess what?" I called brightly. "Some friends from my old school in New York are coming to visit for New Year's. Suzanne and Brendan and Thomas and Mandy." I deliberately gave him the names in that order so that it sounded like two couples. Inspired by this, I went on. "So that means I won't be able to come to the cabin with you."

"You won't be there for New Year's?" Rich said. He looked crushed. "I was really looking forward to it—toasting marshmallows and taking you out to see

145

the moon shining over the mountains at midnight."

"I know," I said, biting my lip. "I was looking forward to it, too. My friends completely surprised me by calling on Christmas Day and inviting themselves."

"They must have a lot of money to be able to afford to fly out just like that."

I nodded. "They're all pretty rich. You know, doctors' kids, lawyers' kids."

"Why don't you bring them up to the cabin? They might enjoy it."

I shook my head hastily. Brendan and Rich in the same cabin? "I don't think so. They're all typical New Yorkers. They expect to be able to do things like go out for a cappuccino at two A.M."

"Out for a what?"

"A coffee," I corrected myself.

"And they're allowed to walk around the city at two A.M.?"

"Some of them are. My parents were always too strict."

"I should think so," he said. "I'd never let my kid wander around New York at two A.M."

"Anyway," I continued, "they'll find it very strange here. I'll try to keep them entertained, but I might not be seeing too much of you while they're here. I hope you understand. They'll want my dad to show them Yellowstone or take them to Jackson Hole—all the touristy things."

He nodded. "It's okay. I understand. I'm glad you're going to get to see your friends again. They

146

must be nice to want to come surprise you like this," he said, sounding a bit disappointed.

"And it's only for a few days," I said. "We have the whole winter to watch the moon shining down on the snow."

"I'm counting on it," he said, his eyes warm as they looked into mine. He reached out and touched my cheek softly before he took off.

"Bye, Rich," I said.

He waved as he disappeared over the hill. I stared after him. How could I possibly want anybody else? How could I risk hurting him? But it was too late.

A couple of days later we drove into Cody to meet Brendan, Suzanne, Mandy, and Thomas. A Greyhound bus had picked them up at the airport—an hour away—and dropped them off in town. Suzanne and Mandy disembarked first. In their long black wool coats and sleek leather boots they looked like ultra-hip New Yorkers—and incredibly out of place. Thomas followed in a new ski outfit, which also stood out from the locals' habitual denims and flannel shirts.

Brendan was last. He was as gorgeous as ever, and I felt my heart do a flip when I saw him. He looked tall and lean and mature in his black leather jacket and casually draped plaid scarf. So much for wondering if I still had feelings for him. I could feel my heart pounding through my thick jacket.

All four of them looked around in disbelief. "There she is!" Suzanne yelled, and they ran toward me. As Brendan's gaze met mine his whole face was lit by his gorgeous smile.

147

"Amber," he said as he took my hands in his, "I can't believe I'm really here. You look so great. I was afraid you might have changed or something, but you look just the same. Actually, you look better than I remembered."

"I've only been gone three months," I said, laughing nervously. I was totally overwhelmed with the delight of being with him again. "Did you expect my hair to have turned gray, or what?"

He laughed with me. His hands were warm and firm as they grasped mine, and I felt shock waves travel right up my arms. By then the others had reached us and were clustering around, yelling and screaming as they tried to hug me.

"I can't believe we finally made it," Suzanne shrieked. "After all this time."

"Amber, you're wearing fur!" Mandy said in a shocked voice.

"What, this?" I laughed again. "This is just my grandma's old jacket. Isn't it cool?"

"But it's fur. Nobody in New York wears fur anymore."

"Hey, it's old and it's been dead a long time. It's only rabbit, for Pete's sake," I said, still amused.

"Even rabbits have feelings, you know," Mandy said. "How would you like it if someone killed you and skinned you just to put you on their back?"

"Not very much," I said. "But rabbits are only raised for meat and fur. They wouldn't have been alive if someone hadn't bred them."

"Boy, I think the ranchers out here have already brainwashed her," Thomas said.

148

"Okay, so I won't wear the fur jacket again," I said.

"Don't mind us, we're only exhausted," Suzanne said. "What a journey. We felt like we were heading for the North Pole. All that way on a bus! Doesn't anybody fly out here?"

"Not many people," I admitted.

"I can see why," Mandy commented, looking around at beautiful downtown Cody. "Amber, you won't believe the places we've come through. Talk about primitive! We stopped at this roadside diner. I asked for a double mocha and a bagel with cream cheese, and the man behind the counter looked at me like I was a creature from Mars."

"They are pretty basic around here," I agreed.

"And this place—talk about dead. Where are the movie theaters? Where are the restaurants? There's nobody here, Amber," Thomas said accusingly. "Where is Jackson Hole? Where are the beautiful people?"

"It's not tourist season," I defended. "Most places close for the winter."

"What do you do with yourself?" Suzanne asked. "I'd go crazy out here."

"Especially without bagels," Mandy agreed.

"We manage to keep busy," I said. "There are tons of chores on the ranch."

My friends looked amused. "Yeah, right," Mandy said.

"What? You don't believe I do chores?"

"Like what?" Brendan asked.

"Feed the cattle, collect the eggs, chop wood—you

name it, I've done it. I told you in my letters," I said, feeling my blood rising.

"We thought you were just putting us on," Suzanne said.

"Well, I wasn't. I do them all."

"What on earth for?" Thomas asked, giving Mandy a sideways look. "You actually like doing stuff like that? I'd have the farmhands do all the hard work."

"The only farmhands we have are my family," I said. "We have to do it all. It was rough at first, when my grandpa still had his cast on, because he was the only person who really knew what he was doing. But we've gotten pretty good at most things."

I saw them looking at each other in pity and surprise.

"It sounds awful," Brendan said. "You must really hate it here. And I can't believe that your parents are enjoying it too much, either. Maybe we can take you back with us!"

I shrugged. "My parents *love* it here," I said. "My mom's baking and quilting, and my dad's writing his novel and taking care of the herd. My brother loves school now, and my sister's going to get a pet lamb. I'd say they're all really happy."

"Oh, Amber, that's terrible," Suzanne said. "So it really does look like you're stuck here. Maybe we can convince your parents to let you come back and stay with one of us."

"I don't think so," I said hastily. "Besides," I added, "I've already promised the cheerleading team that I'll help them make the finals of the state tournament, and I can't let them down."

"State cheerleading tournament?" Mandy and Suzanne looked at each other and burst out laughing. "You—a cheerleader?"

"It's the only winter sport for girls at our school," I said defensively. "And it's the only way I get to practice gymnastics."

"But cheerleading is so sexist," Mandy said. "Amber, where is your car? I'm freezing to death."

"Sorry," I said. "It's over here."

I headed to Grandpa's battered old van, which we used because it had better snow tires.

"Do you have to drive to school in that?" Thomas asked.

"No. I go on the bus," I said.

"On the bus? On a school bus with all those ranch kids? Don't they smell of manure and cows?"

"Actually, they all have running water in their houses."

I was beginning to feel annoyed by their attitude, but also a little guilty too. I knew I'd sounded like that, too, when I first got to Wyoming.

My dad got out of the van to shake hands and help them load their stuff in the back. Brendan climbed into the front seat beside me and slipped his arm around my shoulders, giving me a wink as I looked up at him. It set my heart racing again. Brendan was really there, sitting next to me. After all those months of dreaming, my dreams had finally come true. I knew I should be feeling totally happy and excited, but instead Rich's face under a cowboy hat kept flashing into my mind.

151

The other three got into the back, huddling together in the cold. "Now do you see why I wear fur?" I couldn't resist saying.

They made a big thing of all the bumps and potholes in the road and how far it was and how cold they were, in between telling me all the latest news from school. The production of *A Midsummer Night's Dream* had been fabulous. The fairies' costumes had had Mylar wings, and from the audience it had looked as if they were really flying. It had even been written up in the *New York Times,* and several Broadway actors had gone to opening night.

Suddenly Suzanne let out a yell. My dad swerved and nearly went off the road. "What is it?" he asked.

"That view ahead—the mountains. It's fabulous! Just like the Swiss Alps."

"That's where we live," I said proudly. "I have that view from my bedroom window."

"I'd love a view like that from my bedroom window—if there was a deli on the corner and a movie theater down the block," Mandy said. That time we all laughed.

As we bounced over the snow-covered road I sneaked a look at Brendan. I couldn't believe he was there beside me. And I couldn't believe I was doing this to Rich!

Chapter Fifteen

As we drove up Indian Valley toward our house, they stopped complaining and began to get more enthusiastic. The girls oohed and aahed about the horses in the fields and the cute cabins and the bridges over the stream. Everything looked like a Christmas-card scene to them. I was holding my breath as we turned up the driveway toward our house. It was very important to me that they like it.

"Is that it?" Suzanne asked.

"Yes."

"It's wonderful," Suzanne said. "So quaint, like something out of a Disney movie."

"Yeah, it's the sort of place I'd expect seven dwarves to live in," Mandy chimed in. At that moment the front door opened and Beau came out, wearing a knitted cap on his head.

"There's one of them now," Brendan said, and we

were all laughing crazily as we pulled up in the driveway. I was like a person coming out of a dream. I was beginning to remember how much fun I'd had with Brendan, all the crazy things we'd laughed about. I remembered sitting beside him in biology class while he whispered the most terrible and funny things in my ear and those afternoons at Fiorelli's when I'd sat there entranced, just happy to be listening to him and watching him. I hadn't laughed like that in a long while. It just seemed like my sense of humor wasn't tuned in to the kinds of things that made kids laugh out there in Wyoming.

My family came streaming out of the front door to welcome my friends, looking ridiculously like a family from *Little House on the Prairie*. My mom was even wearing an apron.

"You'll excuse me if I don't hug you, but my hands are all floury," she said. "I just wanted to get some muffins in the oven."

Suzanne dug me in the ribs. "You weren't kidding, were you?" she whispered. "She looks like she's in some Pillsbury Bake-off."

I took them straight upstairs with their stuff. "We've put Brendan and Thomas up in the attic," I said, "and you two can share my room with me."

I saw Mandy and Suzanne looking around my bare little room. "Okay," they said.

"We've got mattresses you can put on the floor, so you'll be out of the draft," I added. "C'mon, I'll show you guys up to the attic."

I led them up the steep stairs to the little room at the front.

154

"Boy, it's freezing up here," Thomas said.

"Yeah, sorry about that. The central heating doesn't get this far. My dad has a little electric heater for when he's writing. You can turn that on," I said.

Brendan pulled me close to him. "Maybe you can sneak up here after everyone's gone to sleep and keep me warm," he whispered.

"Let me warn you that my grandfather hears everything in this house," I said, laughing nervously.

"Hey, Amber," Mandy called as we came downstairs again. "Which bathroom is ours?"

"The room at the end of the hallway. It's the only bathroom we've got."

"For everyone?"

"'Fraid so."

"How do you survive?" Suzanne asked. "We have to kidnap her from here, guys. This is child abuse."

"I've gotten used to it," I said. "It's so cold in the bathroom you won't want to hang around in there anyway."

"I'm glad we're not staying too long," Mandy said. Then she blushed. "I don't mean that I'm not happy to see you, Amber, but you have to admit that this is really roughing it."

Suzanne was already going through my wardrobe. "So what have you bought since you got here? Where do you do your shopping?"

"I haven't really bought anything," I said.

"No new clothes in three months? I'd die. I'd just shrivel up and die," Suzanne said. "Mandy got the most heavenly dress for the winter formal. It cost

155

three hundred dollars and it looked fantastic."

"What there was of it," Brendan said dryly, exchanging one of his famous looks with me.

Suzanne had wandered across to the window and suddenly let out an excited scream. "Look, out there. It's a real cowboy!"

Rich was riding across his family's land, dressed, in spite of the weather, only in a denim jacket and jeans. That guy never seemed to feel the cold! Mandy pushed Suzanne out of the way to get a better view. "Wow, talk about the strong, silent type."

"You mean the strong, stupid type. It's got to be thirty below. I bet they don't exactly go in for brain-power out here. Their conversation is probably limited to 'My cow's bigger than your cow'—right, Amber?"

They all started laughing at that.

"They're steers," I said flatly.

"What?" Four surprised faces looked at me.

"Those animals you saw on the way in. They're male, not female."

"Well, excuse us, Miss Ranchette," Suzanne said, and they all started laughing again.

"So do you know the hunk on the horse?"

"Of course," I said. "I know everybody around here. His name's Rich Winter and he goes to my school."

"You have to introduce us," Mandy said. "I've always wanted to have a romance with a cowboy. Maybe you can take us to a square dance or something and we can do-si-do together, whatever that is."

156

"I can just see you square dancing," Thomas said. "You'd turn the wrong way and bump into everybody."

"I would not. I'm very graceful on my feet. Everyone said I made a divine fairy in the play," Mandy said.

I felt a pang of jealousy. The divine fairy should have been me.

"It's okay, we don't need to go square dancing," Brendan interrupted. "The cowboy is heading this way."

Mandy and Suzanne fought each other to get down the stairs first. I hung back, not knowing what to do next, and Brendan took the opportunity to trap me on the little landing halfway down. "I hope you and I are going to get some time to ourselves," he whispered. "My parents would let me come only if the others came, too, so I didn't have a choice. I hope they're not going to wreck our time together." He was pressing me against the wall, his hand on the wall beside my face, his face inches from mine. "Maybe you can fix up Suzanne and Mandy with the cowboy and his faithful companion, and find Thomas a cowgirl. Then we'll be left in peace."

Confused thoughts raced through my head. Brendan's closeness was disturbing me. I remembered what it had felt like when he kissed me, and part of me wanted to feel his lips on mine again. And Rich was about to walk through that front door any second and see us.

"Brendan, not here," I whispered. "My grandfather will see us or hear us."

"So? Who cares? What am I, Frankenstein's monster?"

I wished he hadn't said that. All of a sudden I had a picture of Rich striding across the field doing his monster impersonation that first day he'd helped me with all the chores. The day we'd fallen in love. Why had I ever thought I could carry this off? It was the world's dumbest idea. It wasn't just a case of juggling two boys and keeping them apart from each other. It was a case of juggling the two halves of my heart.

I broke away from Brendan's hold as Rich's shadow filled the doorway. How was I supposed to act around both guys? Should I kiss Rich hello and have my friends ask tons of questions later? Or should I just stay away and hurt his feelings?

"Howdy," he said, tipping his hat in real cowboy style to my friends. "You must be the visitors from New York that Amber was telling me about. Mary Jo called and said she'd seen the van heading this way, full of people, so I figured it must be you."

"See, he's not so stupid," I heard Mandy whisper to Suzanne.

Suzanne had already stepped forward. "Hi, I'm Suzanne," she said, "and these three weirdos are Mandy, Thomas, and Brendan."

"Gee, thanks a lot, Suzanne," Mandy snapped. "If anyone's the weirdo, you are."

"I'm Rich. I'm . . . uh . . . Amber's neighbor," he said, looking uncomfortable as they crowded around him.

"We know. We saw you galloping across the fields like the Lone Ranger," Suzanne said. "You'll have to show us how you rope cows and all that fun stuff. We've all seen *City Slickers*, you know."

158

Rich looked across at me and gave me an amused look.

"We don't do much roping in the winter," he said. "It's too hard on the horses and it's not much fun to land on your face in the ice and snow, either."

"So what do you do for fun around here?" Suzanne asked pointedly. "We haven't seen a single movie theater or dance club since we left New York."

Rich nodded in agreement. "No, we're a little lacking in the culture department around here. Of course, they have a lot of culture at places like Jackson. But that's too far to drive from here. We mostly make our own fun." And again he looked at me with a secret smile. That was when I knew my plan had worked. Rich thought Suzanne and Thomas, Mandy and Brendan were two couples who'd come to visit me. He didn't feel threatened at all.

"Like what?" Thomas asked.

"Like, for example, we all go up to Mary Jo's cabin in the mountains for New Year's. We have a lot of crazy fun—snowball fights and sledding and singing around a big fire at night. . . ."

"Sounds cool," Suzanne said.

"You're welcome to come along if you like," Rich said. "I told Amber that, but she didn't seem to think it would be your kind of thing."

"Personally I'd love to go," Mandy said. "I think it would be a really different way to spend New Year's Eve."

"Me too," Suzanne said. "It sounds totally cool and romantic."

Rich spread his hands. "Okay, fine with me. I'll

tell Mary Jo and the others you're all coming. We can drive up in my truck, if some of you don't mind sitting out in the back. It's pretty cold, but we bring rugs and it's not a long trip."

"We don't mind at all," Suzanne said—she who, an hour earlier, had been the one to complain loudest about freezing to death in our van. "It sounds great!"

"That's settled, then," Rich said. "Tomorrow afternoon. We'll leave around three to make sure we get up there before dark. Bring warm clothes."

I was the only one who'd said nothing. I was trying desperately to think of something to say that would make them change their minds—such as warning them about man-eating grizzly bears that often attacked lonely cabins, avalanches that buried people alive, or even bug-infested bedding. But the way that Suzanne and Mandy were acting just then, they'd have seen all of those things as just more exotic elements to brag about when they got home: "And then we were attacked by a grizzly bear, right before the avalanche . . ." And I also got the feeling that scoring with a cowboy like Rich was another thing they were determined to brag about.

I looked from Rich's tanned, muscled body to Brendan's expensive hand-knitted sweater, and I swallowed nervously. Both of them in a small cabin at the same time? There was no way I'd be able to keep the truth from coming out. No way at all.

160

Chapter Sixteen

THE NEXT DAY I seriously considered coming down with a mysterious sickness and letting them go to the cabin without me. It seemed to be the only way I could escape the doom that was about to fall. Why had I ever believed I could get away with it? I didn't want to hurt Rich and I didn't want to hurt Brendan. I wanted the impossible. I had fallen in love with the idea of having Rich right there, taking me on moonlight rides, and Brendan back in New York, pining for me and waiting to take me to foreign movies when I got back. Now that they were both flesh-and-blood people, I realized what I'd done. I was going to have to choose between them—between the old Amber and the new.

I paced up and down my room, staring out at the snow-covered fields. I didn't really want to stay in Wyoming, did I? I still dreamed of being back in New

161

York, of shopping in all those stores and going to cafés and plays. And if I went back, I'd want to have Brendan waiting for me. But there was no way I could hurt Rich. . . . It had only just hit me how selfish I'd been. I had been really flattered at the thought of two gorgeous guys fighting over me. It had seemed exciting and dangerous to play one against the other and to try to keep them apart. But I finally saw that it wasn't a game. Serious feelings were involved. The game I was playing was with people's hearts.

The day passed smoothly enough. After lunch my friends took out the toboggans while I drove with my mom to the nearest store to buy supplies for our cabin adventure. We were coming out of the store, bags piled high with goodies, when I saw Rich crossing the parking lot on his way to the store.

"Hey, Rich, if you're going to get hot chocolate, don't bother," I called. "I already have enough for the whole world."

I had expected him to grin, but instead he gave me a cold look. "I prefer to take care of my own needs, thank you," he said.

"What?" I said, confused. I started to walk toward him.

"And while I've got you here, do you want me to go buy a black cap for this afternoon?"

"A black cap? What are you talking about?"

"I mean for when I have to act as chauffeur to you and your friends."

"Rich, what's with you?"

162

He was looking at me with cold, hard eyes. "You can't guess?" he said. "Oh, I suppose that I'm being just a dumb old cowboy. What do I know about the way things are done in New York City? Maybe two-timing is just fine there."

"Rich, please tell me what's wrong," I begged.

"I just thought that I mattered to you, that's all."

"Of course you matter."

"Then you didn't have to lie to me. 'Oh, Rich, here are some friends who came to visit.' Not 'This is my real boyfriend. The one who really matters. The one I really care about.'"

"Rich, where did you hear that?"

"It doesn't matter," he snapped. "I don't want to talk about it anymore. I'll drive you up to the cabin, but then you stay away from me. I thought I could trust you, Amber. But I was wrong."

He started to walk away. "Rich, that isn't fair," I said. "And those things you heard aren't even true. Please let me explain. Rich, please!"

But he'd gone. I stood there staring after him. I couldn't stand to see that look of hurt on his face. I'd have done anything in the world to make it right, but I didn't know what to do.

My mother appeared beside me. "Come on, honey, let's go home," she said. "There's nothing you can do right now. His pride has been hurt."

"I didn't want to hurt him, Mom," I said. "And I don't want to lose him."

"I told you it was a big risk, letting Brendan come here," Mom chided. "I told you that you might have

163

to choose between them—and hurt one of them in the process. And now you have."

"Okay. Fine," I snapped. "I'm already feeling bad enough. Don't make me feel worse. I just want to know who's responsible for telling him and wrecking my life. That's all my family is good for, wrecking my life again and again."

I stomped ahead of her to the van and sat in stony silence all the way home. I couldn't get Rich's hurt look out of my mind. For the first time it really hit me that I had power over another human being—power to make him happy or to hurt him. And that when you hurt a special person, a person you really care about a lot, it hurts you too.

My friends were sprawled around the fire as I came into the house.

"Amber, what does frostbite look like in its early stages?" Brendan called. "I think one of my fingers is about to fall off."

I went on through to the kitchen and started unpacking groceries. Suzanne came out to join me. "Guess what?" she said. "I went out for a little walk and I bumped into your hunky cowboy again. We had a long talk. It was lucky we did, because you'll never guess what he thought. He thought that Brendan and I were an item."

I opened my mouth, but no sound came out. Suzanne kept right on babbling excitedly. "I had to set him straight on that one right away. I told him that Brendan had never looked at anyone except you, and that you two couldn't wait to get back together again.

I told him how you'd called each other every night and how you just fell into each other's arms when he got off the bus and how positively annoying it was to watch you gaze into each other's eyes and sigh." She was laughing. "Then I told Rich that *I* was as free as a bird, if he didn't have a special girl at the moment. And he said he was as free as a bird, too. Isn't that great?"

"Oh, sure, Suzanne. Absolutely wonderful. Thanks a million," I said.

"What's with you?"

"You've just blown my chance at happiness, that's all."

"You mean, you and the cowboy?" she asked suspiciously.

"I didn't realize how much I cared about him," I blurted out, only understanding the words as I spoke them. "And now I've lost him, Suzanne. I've really hurt him, and I don't know what to do."

"What about Brendan?" Suzanne said, glancing back into the other room. "I thought you were still pining for him."

"I thought I was, too," I said, "until he got here and I realized that I'd changed. Brendan is great, and I was so flattered that he liked me, but Rich has become really special to me. And now I've hurt him."

Suzanne put her hand on my shoulder. "I'm sorry, Amber. I had no idea. How could I have? You never said anything."

"I know. It's totally my fault. I guess I was just flattered by the thought of two guys liking me. I thought I could handle this—you know, like Miss Cool—and have a chance to see which guy I liked best. I never thought about what it would do to the guys. I never believed a guy's heart could break." I sank onto the kitchen chair. "What am I going to do, Suzanne?"

"Wait until we've left and then explain the whole thing to Rich."

"That will look like I'm giving him second prize," I moaned. "'Brendan's gone home, so now you're number one with me again.' He wouldn't want that."

"Then you have to find a way to convince him he's number one."

"But that would hurt Brendan. He's come all this way to see me, Suzanne. I don't want to hurt him, either."

Suzanne shrugged. "Don't ask me. I'm not Dear Abby," she said. "And I kind of wanted your cowboy for myself."

I decided we wouldn't go to the cabin that night. I'd say the road was blocked and the trip had to be canceled at the last moment. But Rich's mother blew that little plan by calling up to say that Rich would be over at two-thirty sharp and wanted to make sure we were all ready.

I grabbed my mother as she was packing our groceries into a carton. "Mom, do you think it would be the worst thing in the world if I didn't go with them?" I asked. "I could tell everyone I wasn't feeling well."

She looked at me. "Of course you have to go, Amber. They're your guests and it's up to you to entertain them. They're really looking forward to this cabin thing, but they won't know anybody. Besides, Mary Jo's parents will be there, and they've got an entire itinerary planned. You won't have time to be alone with either boy."

"But I can't face it, Mom. I can't stand the thought of being up there with Brendan and Rich."

She shrugged. "You set up this situation, Amber. I'm afraid you'll just have to handle it," she said. "It's only for one night and there will be a big group of kids. I don't see why you have to have a dramatic confrontation with either of them."

It struck me that she wasn't taking the whole thing very seriously. "You think this is funny, don't you?" I demanded.

"No. It's not at all funny," she said. "But it's not the end of the world, you know."

I don't think I'd ever felt more alone.

If I can just keep my cool for this one night, I thought, *I'll ask Dad to drive them to Yellowstone for the rest of their trip. I'll tell Brendan the truth. And then I'll go to Rich and grovel, throwing myself at his feet and begging him to take me back.*

Rich pretended he didn't notice me as I walked past him and threw my sleeping bag into the back of the truck. I climbed in after it and let Mandy and Suzanne have the seat beside Rich. Maybe a miracle would happen and Suzanne would tell Rich that she'd gotten it all wrong, that I'd never liked Brendan after all. But then I remembered that Suzanne wanted Rich for herself. She had never been good at sharing and she always got what she wanted in the end.

We set off up the valley, the truck bouncing and

167

sliding over the packed snow. It had snowed heavily two nights earlier, and the world had turned into a series of unrecognizable humps and bumps. Only the cattle stood out as little brown dots against the snowy landscape. Soon we left the fields behind and the road started to zigzag upward. The pine trees were weighted down with their blankets of snow, and nothing moved in the silent landscape. The sun was already setting behind distant hills, and soon we plunged into deep shadow. It was too cold to talk. Brendan and Thomas and I all sat huddled together with the sleeping bags and blankets around us, the scarves pulled over our faces making us look like bandits.

"There *will* be a fire at this cabin, won't there?" Thomas muttered.

"Will there be a doctor who knows how to treat frostbite?" Brendan quipped. "I hope he doesn't have to take off all my fingers." He slipped his arm around my shoulders and pulled me close to him. "You and I will just have to spend the night wrapped in each other's arms, Amber. I'm sure your parents will understand that we did it for survival!"

I was sure Rich had seen us through the back window. "Brendan, don't!" I said, and shrugged him off. "You're pushing the blanket off my shoulders," I added. I wanted to feel cold and miserable. I wanted to suffer the way Rich was suffering.

We continued to climb.

"Where is this cabin—at the top of Mount McKinley?" Thomas shouted.

His voice echoed, unnaturally loud and magnified, from the cliff walls above us.

"Hey, listen to that," Thomas said, pleased with himself. "I'm powerful! Hellooo out there!" Then he started a horrible attempt at yodeling.

As if in answer, there was a deep, booming crash and a rumble far above us.

"What was that?" Thomas asked nervously. "Is someone shooting at us?"

"Maybe they didn't like the sound of your voice," Brendan said. "Can't say I blame them."

Rich must have heard it, too. Having been born in those mountains, he knew what it meant. Suddenly he put his foot down on the accelerator and drove like crazy. We were bumping, lurching, and skidding all over the place.

"Has the cowboy flipped? What's he doing?" Brendan shouted.

I looked up the hill and then I understood. What looked like a line of white dust was speeding down the mountain toward us, engulfing trees as it came.

"An avalanche," I gasped. "Rich must be trying to outrun it."

"He's crazy. Look how fast it's moving."

"Better than sitting here waiting for it to hit us," I said through chattering teeth.

The engine roared in protest as Rich gunned it up the steep track. But soon we couldn't hear the engine anymore because of the rumbling roar above us. Chunks of ice, ahead of the main wall of snow, hit the side of the truck. Brendan pulled me down under the sleeping bag. I couldn't take my eyes off the approaching snow. It was beautiful and terrifying at the same time, like a giant creature with a life of its own.

For a while it looked as if Rich really would be able to outrun it, but the very edge of the flow struck the back of the truck as it crashed past, covering us with snow and sending us into a crazy spin down the mountain. Rich gunned the engine once more as we were pulled backward. The wheels spun, screeched, and finally came to rest against a tree as the white destruction plunged onward, down to the valley.

Chapter Seventeen

NOBODY MOVED. I think we were all convinced that the truck would topple down the hill if anyone dared to speak. Then slowly, one by one, we climbed out, standing on the steep slope and looking at the trees snapped like matchsticks beside us. My teeth started chattering again. It wasn't easy to accept that we'd been inches from death.

"Is everyone okay?" Rich asked shakily, his eyes on me.

"What do we do now?" Suzanne asked. "How do we get the truck back onto the road?"

Rich shrugged. "It would take a heavy winch. They'll have to bring one up from the valley."

He looked at the wall of debris that now closed the road behind us.

"So what are we going to do?" Suzanne insisted. "We'll freeze if we just stand here."

Rich looked up the track and then back, as if thinking.

"I don't think I could get back to the nearest house by nightfall," he said. "We could try camping out in the truck until someone finds us."

"Are you crazy?" Brendan demanded. "It was freezing in the back of that truck."

"It might be the best we can do," Rich said. "The golden rule is never to leave your vehicle if you want to be spotted."

"But what about the cabin we were going to?" Mandy asked.

Rich shook his head. "It's far. It will be dark soon and it's easy to miss the turn in the darkness. If we walked past it, there's nothing else."

"Well, you brought us here, cowboy, you go for help," Mandy snapped. "You're supposed to know what to do. We're not used to stuff like this."

"Yeah, Rich. You had no right bringing us up here if you knew there was going to be an avalanche," Suzanne told him.

"And there's no way we'd survive a night in this truck," Brendan said. "We couldn't all fit inside the cab. And I, for one, am not volunteering to stay in the back."

They were all looking at Rich defiantly. Rich frowned as he tried to decide what to do. "There is a little hut somewhere around here," he said. "My dad uses it sometimes. Maybe we should try and get there before dark."

"How far is it?" Suzanne asked.

"About two miles, maybe."

"Two miles?" Mandy yelled. "You expect me to walk two miles in Italian designer boots?"

"Then stay in the truck if you want," Rich said.

I thought he was keeping his cool really well.

"You know, you're in big trouble," Thomas said shakily. "You risked our lives bringing us up here. My dad's a lawyer."

"So sue me if you make it down safely," Rich said angrily. "Only just keep your voices down, if you don't want to start another avalanche."

I gave Thomas a hard stare—and his face turned bright red. For the first time he began to realize that maybe his yelling had started the whole thing.

"Okay, let's get started walking, or we'll never find this hut before it gets really dark," Rich said.

"This is so stupid," Mandy whined. "I'll wreck these boots if I walk through deep snow in them."

I hadn't said a thing, partly because I had been so shocked, but partly because I felt I was in the middle. I wanted to be on Rich's side, but these were my guests. I could understand that they were freaked out. I was freaked out, and I'd had three months to get used to the place. But suddenly enough was enough. They were blaming Rich for an avalanche that one of them had probably started. They were blaming him when most probably he had saved their lives.

"Give it a break, you guys," I said. "You're lucky to be alive. If Rich hadn't used his head and driven so well, we'd be under all that snow at the bottom of the hill by now." I picked up my sleeping bag and my backpack. "Come on, let's get started. If we don't, we'll never find it in the dark."

"I just hope Rich knows where he's going," Suzanne muttered, grabbing her stuff from the back of the truck. "And someone had better bring the hot chocolate."

"We'll have to divide up the food stuff," Rich said, taking packets out of the grocery box.

"I already have way too much to carry," Mandy said. "*I* don't have room for the hot chocolate. Besides, we're not used to walking like this."

"Leave some of that stuff in the truck, Mandy," I said. "All you really need for tonight is your sleeping bag and an extra sweater if you have one."

"What about a change of clothes for the morning, Amber?" Mandy said in a horrified voice. "I can't wear the same clothes I've slept in. Get real."

I glanced across at Rich despairingly, and he grinned. For a second it was as if we were totally on the same wavelength and everyone else was an alien. "It's okay. I've got room for a box of hot chocolate," I said. "And quit complaining."

"That's not very nice, Amber," Suzanne said. "We are your guests, after all."

"You wanted to come," I said. "I didn't invite you." I hadn't meant to say it. It just slipped out.

"What?" Suzanne exclaimed. "Well, thanks a lot. We pay all this money to come out here for the vacation from hell and you say you didn't even want us here? Some friend you are."

"I didn't mean it like that, Suzanne," I said, hurry-

174

ing after her up the track, but she wouldn't stop.

We left the main route and started up a narrow logging road, almost invisible under the snow.

"I hope you know where you're going," Brendan said to Rich.

Rich looked at him coldly. "I guess you just have to trust me," he said. "Right now you don't have much choice unless you want to hike back to the valley."

"Wise guy," Brendan grumbled.

Suzanne and Mandy were floundering in the deep snow. They both had on leather boots with pointed toes and little heels. Suzanne tripped and went sprawling. When she got up, she was covered in snow. "I hate this place!" she yelled. "This is the worst place I've ever been in my entire life. It's cold and it's boring and it's full of stupid, idiotic people who can't even drive a truck up a road without getting swept away by an avalanche."

She sounded so funny that I had to swallow a laugh. I glanced across at Rich, but his mouth was set in a hard, straight line.

"Come on, get moving," Rich said, grabbing Suzanne's arm. "We have to get you inside before that snow soaks through." He half dragged her up the trail.

I jumped as Brendan grabbed my arm. "What?" I asked.

He motioned me to be quiet. "Listen," he whispered, "I don't think we're going to make it with Suzanne going as slow as she is. We'll all freeze to death if we stay out here. So how about you and I slip back to the truck? It would be warm enough in the cab, just the two of us."

"No. I don't think so. I can't leave Rich alone with everyone else," I said, surprising myself.

"Sure you can," Brendan said easily. "He got us into this. It's up to him to get us out of it."

I looked at Brendan. What had I found so exciting about him? Out in the backcountry, where he was no longer confident and the star attraction, he wasn't attractive at all. And his whining was beginning to annoy me.

"Out here we don't let down our friends," I said, stalking ahead of him. "Come on, guys," I said, loud enough for everyone to hear as I fell into step beside Rich. "Quit whining. You're acting like a bunch of wimps. You're always looking for someone else to blame. Well, that's not the way life is supposed to be. We have to rely on ourselves out here, so get moving or Rich and I will leave you behind."

I saw Rich give me an appraising look as I passed him. I heard Thomas say, "Well, wooee. Listen to Amber, the pioneer woman." That made everyone laugh, and they started walking faster.

Ahead a dark shape loomed through the trees. "There it is!" I called. We all ran the last few yards to the little hut. It took us a while to break in, but the combined strength of the boys finally busted the lock and we went inside. It smelled damp and musty and there was no light.

"You can't expect us to spend the night in here," Mandy began, but Rich was already rummaging around the shelves. He found matches and newspaper and within minutes a fire blazed up in the hearth.

There was a supply of dry wood stacked in the corner and a primitive bunk bed along one wall. We got Suzanne out of her wet clothes and into a sleeping bag while Rich put on water to boil. There were only three mugs, but for once nobody seemed to mind sharing.

"Do you think we'll have to spend the whole night here?" Mandy asked. "Won't someone come looking for us pretty soon?"

"They'll miss us when we don't show up at the cabin, won't they?" I asked.

Rich shook his head. "They'll just think you guys decided at the last minute not to come. Nobody will be looking for us until morning at the earliest. They won't be able to get up from the valley without a snowplow."

"Oh, my God," Suzanne said. "I hope this doesn't turn out like one of those movies where they're trapped in the snow and they have to start eating people."

Rich and I burst out laughing at the same time.

"Are you volunteering to be first, Suzanne?" I asked sweetly. Now that I was warm and safe again, I was feeling more feisty. I'd just decided that my former friends were annoying the hell out of me. The cabin felt like an adventure to me. I couldn't help thinking how cozy it would have been if I'd been there alone with Rich.

The others were also thawing out and relaxing, making the sort of dumb jokes people make after they've been scared. Rich got up. "I'd better go see if there's more wood hidden somewhere outside," he said. "This batch won't last all night."

As he went out Mandy said, "And while you're out there, be an angel and bring me a cappuccino. I'm dying for cappuccino."

"I'm sorry, ma'am, but I don't think there's any of them things running around in these woods," Rich said. This made all of them laugh and nudge each other about how dumb he was.

I was hot with embarrassment. I knew very well that Rich was playing the backwoods boy for them because that was how they had typed him. I got up and followed him outside. I couldn't see him right away. He had been right about the moonlight, though. It filled the forest with silver brightness, making the snow sparkle like diamonds.

I didn't hear Brendan come up behind me, and I jumped when he put his hand on my shoulder. "Finally, we get to be alone," he whispered. "I was beginning to think I'd never get to be alone with you this whole trip, what with your nosy grandfather and your bratty little sister. But now we have the perfect excuse because we're trying to keep warm."

He tried to pull me close to him, his hands slipping inside my parka, but I shrugged him off. "Brendan, don't," I said firmly.

He was grinning. "Oh, come on, Amber. What's your problem now? You're so uptight—relax."

"I'm sorry, Brendan," I said. "You were nice enough to come visit me and I was just trying to get through your visit without telling you the truth. I . . . I guess I was being a coward, but I really didn't want to hurt your feelings."

Brendan gave a small laugh. "What? Are you trying to tell me you don't want me anymore?"

"I guess so," I said. I took a deep breath and began, "You see—" But before I could finish, he grabbed me.

"This cold air must be affecting your brain." His lips were fumbling for mine, and he was holding me so tightly that it hurt.

"No, Brendan." I pushed him away with all my strength. He went flying backward and landed in the snow. I hadn't realized until then that all those farm chores really had built up my muscles. Brendan looked astonished, and very mad. He staggered up from the snow.

"Boy, have you changed," he growled.

"I'm sorry," I said. "I didn't mean to push you over. But you're right. I have changed. Different things are important to me now." I wanted to say, "Rich is important to me now," but Brendan cut in.

"I saw it right away. You're no fun anymore. You've become just as boring as everyone else up here. I can't wait to get out of this dumb place in the morning."

He stalked back into the hut, slamming the door behind him. I stood there, alone in the night, not knowing what to do next.

"Nice muscles, lady," came a voice from the darkness. "I'm going to enter you in the calf-roping contest next spring."

I turned to see Rich leaning against a big pine tree.

"You saw all that?"

He nodded. "I was just about to come to your rescue, until I saw you didn't need me."

179

"You're wrong," I said. "I do need you."

"Yeah?"

"Yeah," I said, taking a deep breath. "I've been trying to find a way to tell Brendan ever since he got here. I didn't want him to come in the first place, but I was too much of a coward to say so."

Rich's eyes were bright in the moonlight.

"Well, that's not completely true," I went on slowly, because it was hard for me to say it with Rich's eyes staring right into my soul. "I wanted to see if I still had feelings for Brendan. I had such great memories, Rich. I wanted to make sure I was making the right choice."

"And what is the right choice?" he asked steadily.

"That I don't belong with Brendan or any of my New York friends anymore. They don't know what's real."

"And what is real?" he whispered. He was so close to me that I found it hard to think clearly.

"You and me," I whispered. "I think we're very, very real. I didn't realize it until yesterday, Rich. Nothing in my whole life hurt me as much as knowing I'd hurt you. I knew I'd do anything in my power to make things right again."

Slowly his arms stole around me. "I think you just did," he said. His lips were surprisingly warm as they came to meet mine. I don't know how long we stayed there, holding each other tightly, while the snow sparkled around us. When we finally broke apart, Rich laughed. "I suppose we should go inside. It wouldn't be good to be found frozen together like this in the morning."

"I can't think of a better way to go," I said, gazing up at him adoringly.

"Come on," he said, touching my cheek. "Help me carry in some of these logs."

"I only wish we'd come across a pot of steaming cappuccino," I said, laughing. "I'd have loved to see Mandy's face!"

In the morning we woke to the sound of engines roaring. A helicopter was flying low overhead, and we ran down to the main track to meet a snowplow. My parents and various other neighbors were right behind it.

"Thank God you're safe," my dad said, wrapping me in his big arms. "We were so worried when they went to check out the avalanche and reported that they'd seen the truck but no signs of life."

"Oh, don't worry about us," I said, holding Rich's hand tightly. "We had an expert woodsman with us. He took care of us just fine."

"So everything's okay, then?" my mother asked.

"Everything's just wonderful," I said, and I turned to smile at Rich. He leaned over to kiss me. "Actually, it's perfect." So perfect, in fact, that I realized I was looking forward to finishing high school there in Wyoming with my family, with Grandpa . . . and, of course, with Rich.

Do you ever wonder about falling in love? About members of the opposite sex? Do you need a little friendly advice but have no one to turn to? Well, that's where we come in . . . Jenny and Jake. Send us those questions you're dying to ask, and we'll give you the straight scoop on life and love.

DEAR JAKE

Q: *My brother Ethan is two years older than I am and he's very protective of me. We go to the same school and occasionally wind up at the same parties—which totally pisses him off. Last weekend I met a really great guy at one of these parties and it turns out he's one of my brother's friends. I like him a lot, but I know Ethan would kill us both if he found out we were dating. I don't want to ruin my brother's friendship with this guy, but I don't want to miss out on the opportunity to get to know him better. I need a guy's point of view, Jake. What should I do?*

JF, Kansas City, MO

A: Tell your brother to lighten up! He obviously loves you very much and just wants to protect you from the random jerks out there. Ethan probably feels threatened when you both go to the same parties, and doesn't want guys talking about you the way they sometimes do about other girls. I know this is hard to believe, but he's just looking out for your best interests. Let your brother know you plan to date this guy and explain that you're not taking his friend away from him. You're obviously old enough to choose who you want to date. Now you need to convince your brother to trust your judgment. Tell him you'll always value his opinion, but to butt out until you ask for it.

Q: *My friend Mike and I do everything couples do, but he won't ask me out. We go out every weekend together——to the movies, to parties, to football games——but he says he doesn't want a girlfriend right now. I really care about him——and I think he's an absolute hunk. I've just got to do something to make him change his mind about me. Any suggestions?*

MS, Hallandale, FL

A: Right now this guy is getting all the advantages of having a girlfriend with none of the responsibilities (like having to be faithful to one girl), so you're going to have a pretty tough time convincing him to go for a commitment. You need to let him know that you want to have a real relationship. If he runs for the nearest door, he was only using you—and you're better off without him. But if he sticks around, he might simply be scared of commitment. That's your cue to show him why getting seriously involved with you would be more rewarding—especially emotionally—than just being casual friends. Be warm and sensitive, talk to him, and understand that he may be exploring new emotions here. And give him some time to learn to look at you as a girlfriend rather than just one of the guys.

DEAR JENNY

Q: *Paul and I got to know each other when we were teamed together for a class assignment. We had a lot in common and I thought we really hit it off. I decided to slip a note into his locker, telling him that I liked him. But Paul wrote back, saying he wasn't interested. The thing is, recently he's been acting like he is interested. He seems to go out of his way to talk to me in school and he's always hanging out by my locker. What's up with this guy? Does he like me or not?*

AK, South Bend, IN

A: This may be a real eye-opener, but some guys are very traditional and like to make the first move. Maybe your note surprised him, and he reacted without thinking. Now that he's had time to think it over, Paul might realize he really likes you. My advice is to back off a bit, but *definitely* let him know you're still interested. If Paul doesn't respond after a while, chalk it up to the fact that he's just a nice guy who wants to be your friend. Then you can look for someone else who's more in tune with your direct-approach method.

Q: *My boyfriend and I were friends for a year before we started going out. We used to hang out together constantly, talking for hours about everything under the sun. But now that we've officially become a couple, we're surrounded by awkward moments of silence. Is there anything I can do?*

GB, Tuscumbia, AL

A: First thing, don't panic! This breakdown in communication suggests that one or both of you are not as comfortable as you think with your new status as a couple. Maybe you have unrealistic expectations about how radically your relationship should change now that you're official. Great romances are built on great friendships, so don't expect things to be that different now that you're going out. Maybe the two of you should go back to friendship until you each feel comfortable going for more. The odds are in your favor, you just need to work at keeping the friendship alive in your romantic lives.

Do you have questions about love? Write to:

Jenny Burgess or Jake Korman
c/o Daniel Weiss Associates
33 West 17th Street
New York, NY 10011

Watch out Sweet Valley University— the Wakefield twins are on campus!

Jessica and Elizabeth are away at college, with no parental supervision! Going to classes and parties . . . learning about careers and college guys . . . they're having the time of their lives. Join your favorite twins as they become SVU's favorite coeds!